THE
PRINCESS

THE FILTHY TRILOGY BOOK TWO

D1570165

NEW YORK TIMES BESTSELLING AUTHOR
LISA RENEE JONES

ISBN-13: 978-1794399921

CHAPTER ONE

Harper

Darkness engulfs me inside the Kingston warehouse as I try to escape the hand on my mouth and the big body at my back, but then I hear a whispered, "Easy, sweetheart," at my ear and everything familiar about this man washes over me with relief. It's Eric. Oh God, it's Eric. He came back. He's here. He's with me and I have never been so happy to feel someone this close as I am now.

"Shhhh," he murmurs softly and then releases my mouth.

I rotate in his arms and hug him so tightly that it hurts, but somehow it's not tight enough.

He holds onto me, his hand flattening between my shoulder blades, but this is not just about affection. This is him holding me, keeping me still. This is him listening for movement and the necessity of my silence replaces my relief.

We aren't alone.

This wasn't a random power outage.

I stiffen and softly inhale a calming breath. Eric strokes my hair as if in approval and then kisses my temple before pulling me around and then in front of him. His hands go to my shoulders and he starts walking us forward, and I have no sense of where we are in the

1

Kingston warehouse, but somehow he does. I sense this. I know this. I remind myself he's not only a genius but an ex-Navy SEAL. About that moment is when he abruptly stops walking and we just stand there, and stand there, and I swear there is a whisper of movement somewhere nearby.

I don't know where.

I just know it's here. It's close. Someone is with us.

Eric suddenly moves me forward and we take five fast steps before he stops us again. He reaches around me and my hands plant on what I think is a moving door. He walks me inside what I now know is an office, as the aquarium inside the foreman's office glows. He moves quickly then, shutting us inside and moving me into a corner. For the first time since he arrived, I can see him, and even in the shadows, he's beautiful and intense.

"You came back."

"I should never have left," he says, cupping my face. "And we have a lot to talk about when this is over." He kisses me and then takes my hand and presses a gun into it. "Shoot first. Ask questions later." He shrugs out of his jacket and tosses it. "Call 911, but don't move. You could run right into a problem. I'll be right back." He starts to move away.

I catch his arm, my heart lurching as I plead, "Wait. Don't go. You could get hurt."

"I won't get hurt." His hands settle on my shoulders and as if he knows I need to hear the words again, he repeats, "I'll be back. Don't move." He starts to step away again, but suddenly halts, holding a finger to his lips to silence me. I nod and he turns toward the door, silently stepping to a spot that places him behind it as it opens. The next thing I know, Eric and some man in all black are exchanging punches. Eric throws him across the desk and I don't even consider running. I hold the gun ready

CHAPTER THREE

Harper

I grip the arms of my seat as the small private plane lifts off and climbs to the higher altitudes with jolts, jumps, and shakes, with only one thought: *Oh God, please don't let us crash.* I'm terrified and not because I'm an amateur flyer. I'm not. I've flown. I've even flown in bad conditions, but nothing like this, with the plane jerking, violently pulling and pushing, but I can surmise why pretty darn quickly. Pilots don't take off in conditions like this. Eric paid this one, and I suspect paid him well, to get us off the ground. Considering the conditions, I can only assume that he felt it was far more dangerous to stay on the ground than travel in treacherous weather.

We jerk violently to the right and I stop analyzing Eric's reasoning for taking off in this mess. I focus on praying that we survive the powerful gust of wind, tossing us around. The plane seems to hopscotch and my white-knuckled grip tightens right as we jerk sharply left and then drop a good two feet that leaves me gasping.

Eric reaches over the small aisle and grabs my hand, his touch strong and warm. The minute he tightens his grip on me, I breathe out the air trapped in my lungs. I breathe when I thought I couldn't. This man has a way of just crawling inside me and settling there. He's a part of me in ways I have never understood until now. It's like we haven't spent all these years apart.

He rotates his chair to face me when I'm pretty sure it's supposed to be locked down, not rotating. He reaches to the side of my seat, unlocks it, and then rotates me to face him. My seat tries to sway with the bumping of the plane, and he quickly holds onto it while leaning in and locking me back into place. Now we're closer, and thanks to his long legs, our knees touch, while those blue eyes of his fix on my face. His hands settle on my knees. "I've flown through hell and back with a lot less skill controlling the plane. We have a military pilot in control. A man who flew in a combat mission while under heavy fire. He's good. Really damn good."

"Which is why you paid him to take off in *really* bad weather," I say and I can't keep the accusation from my tone.

"Yes," he says. "Exactly."

We rock and sway. I grab his hands, but he switches our hands and presses mine to my legs, covering them with his. "We're safe."

"You paid him to take off when he normally wouldn't because you thought we'd get murdered on the ground."

"He wouldn't have taken off if he thought it was too dangerous. He goes down with us, remember?"

"I see how you avoided the part about us getting murdered. And as for the pilot, people do crazy things for money."

"Money does him no good if he's dead. He goes down if we go down," he repeats. "Let's talk and get your mind off the flight."

"I'm *not t*alking about what we need to talk about while fearing for my life."

"All right then. We have four hours in the air. Let's start with something simpler."

"Define simpler," I say cautiously, and the weather seems to answer, the plane leveling out, nice and steady.

"You wanted to know about my tattoos. Let's talk about my tattoos." He releases me and starts rolling up his sleeves, displaying his incredibly intricate ink as he does. It distracts me. It has my attention, right up until the moment that the plane jerks again. I jump and Eric grabs my legs again. "I got you."

He has me. He does. I know that, but for how long? How long until this man is gone? How long until he breaks my heart? Because he will and yet when I'm with him I can't seem to care.

"I got you," he says again, his eyes warm. I'm warm too now. "I did a horrible job of showing you that tonight but I'll you'll know soon. I'll show you."

"I don't know what to say to that," I whisper.

"Say you believe me. Say you trust me."

"Say *you* trust *me*," I demand. "You didn't trust me when Isaac of all people got in between us."

His reply is to hold out his arm, displaying his powerful forearm and colorful ink. "Ask me anything, Harper."

My gaze rockets to his and for a moment, I study that handsome, rugged face, looking for the meaning behind his offer and what I find is vulnerability. These tattoos are more than ink to him. He's told me this. They're his life. They're his secrets. They're a look into his soul. He's offering me a window into that soul and trusting me not to abuse it.

My attention immediately settles on his left arm, on the rows of numbers banding its width, and stacking on top of each other, some with images and others without. I run my fingers over a row of nothing but numbers. "This one," I say, looking at him again. "What does this one mean?"

"It says, 'everyone has a price.'"

My lips tighten. "You mean me."

"Everyone, Harper, not just you, but the truth is, that you, at least in part, inspired that tattoo."

My gut clenches, throat tightens. He still thinks that I stayed at Kingston for power and money.

"I know why you stayed. You've paid a price and that price was years of your life."

"To protect my father's creation, his empire." I swallow hard. "His memory."

"I told you," he replies softly. "I know why you stayed and I get it. I stayed for a long time, too. I wanted to be a Kingston but the price for me became too high."

"Was there a price you paid for leaving?"

"You. I left you behind, but no matter how many regrets I have about that now, that was how it had to be then, Harper. I didn't know me like I do now. I wasn't the man I am now."

I think of my miscarriage, and how that baby wasn't meant to be, but I wanted it to be. I wanted it badly. I swallow hard and look at another tattoo, a grim reaper with numbers next to it. "This one," I say, before it hits me that this could be about his mother, but it's too late. I've committed to the question, and he's told me to ask anything. "What does it mean?" I ask, meeting his stare.

"You would pick that right now, wouldn't you?" he teases.

"If you don't want to talk about it—"

"Tuus mors, mea vita," he says. Latin for 'your death, my life.'"

His mother.

I was right.

This is about his mother.

I swallow hard, feeling a punch of emotion for the young man who lost a parent and so very brutally. "What does it mean to you, Eric?"

"It's meant a lot of things to me at different times in my life, but ultimately 'kill or be killed' is the meaning it's taken on in my later years. It's about survival."

I accept this answer. Maybe I was wrong. Maybe it wasn't about his mother at all. "Did you get it when you were in the Navy?" I ask.

"No. You can't tell now, since it's surrounded by the rest of my ink, but it was one of my first tattoos. I got it after my mother committed suicide." He glances skyward and seems to struggle with what he is about to say before he fixes me in a turbulent stare. "My mother wrote those words to me in her suicide note. *My death. Your life.*"

Emotion balls in my throat. "I'm sorry I chose that tattoo."

"I'm not," he says, squeezing my hand. "You want to know me, you have to know her and how she affected who I am. Harper, I protect myself but I also protect those I care about, the way she did. She protected me. She made the ultimate sacrifice for me. When another person would have fought for a cure to cancer, for more life, she fought for me. The way I'm fighting for you. You just don't know it yet and with good reason. I haven't shown you, but I will. I am. Wait and see."

The plane shakes and then immediately enters calmer air once more. The plane is steady, the flying smooth, but I'm in knots. His mother died. He has no real family left, but I was carrying his child. I don't know what that means to him but it meant, it *means*, so very much to me. It's time to talk. We have to have this conversation no matter what the outcome. We have to talk about the child we lost.

LISA RENEE JONES

CHAPTER FOUR

Harper

Suddenly, I'm the one jumping subjects and driving us to the place I didn't want to go. "I would have called you if I hadn't miscarried. I swear to you, I would have, but what was the point once—once I lost the baby?" I choke up and try to turn away, but my seat is locked and Eric is holding my legs.

I look down at my lap, at our hands, and Eric cups my face, forcing my eyes to his. "Tell me. Tell me everything. Forget you said anything on my voicemail. I want to hear it from you."

"What did Isaac tell you?"

"It doesn't matter what Isaac told me. It matters what you tell me."

"Because I didn't tell you when it happened?"

"You told me why. I understand why."

"Mostly on voicemail, though. I didn't know if you would believe the baby was yours, and it was. I hadn't been with anyone else. And I thought you'd think I had some Kingston agenda for telling you when you could do nothing to change what happened." The plane shudders a moment, as if warning me to stop now.

"I might have," he admits. "I don't like to believe that I would have, but I saw you on that stage with the family at the party, and I left believing you were one of them. And that means manipulative and self-serving. In my mind, at that point in my life, I left you before you burned me."

"I know," I whisper, my throat thick. "I know that. I knew that. That was why it just didn't make sense to call you, but I wanted to. You were the only person who it might matter to like it did me. I didn't tell anyone."

"But Isaac knows because he was there when it happened," he confirms.

"Yes."

"Tell me," he urges again, a gentle but forceful push to his voice. "I wasn't there then. Let me be here for you now." He hesitates. "If you can."

I swallow hard. "Yes. I can. You deserve to hear the story, but I want you to know that I was going to tell you. I almost told you back at my house, in my bedroom when we were—when you thought something was wrong—"

"The condom," he supplies, following my lead. "You were thinking about this when I was putting on the condom."

I nod. "Yes, then, and several times that night. God, how I wanted to just tell you, but we kept having visitors and problems come up. I couldn't find just one good moment alone with you that felt like the right time to talk about this."

"I'm here now. *We're* here now."

It's another prod and I don't make him push me harder. "I didn't know I was pregnant. Honestly, I didn't even suspect it. I was late starting my period, but I've had that happen on occasion and I was working long and hard hours."

"You didn't have morning sickness?" he asks.

"Yes, but I didn't know it was morning sickness. I was barely sleeping. I had no reason to suspect I was pregnant. I thought I was just pushing myself too hard. We didn't finish what we started that night. I didn't think

I *could* be pregnant." My lips purse. "Of course, I found out in a brutal way how wrong I was on that." I squeeze my eyes shut and when his fingers brush my cheek, I look at him. "I was cramping, so I thought I was finally going to start my period."

Suddenly I'm back in the past, back in my office, and reliving that night all over again in vivid color.

"I was sitting at my desk, sorting through a stack of files and I couldn't find the one that I needed. Frustrated that I couldn't finish my report without it and finally get out of there, I knew I had to hunt it down or miss the critical deadline for the production department. I stood up and rounded my desk when a punch of cramps hit my belly. I slouched forward as another punch hit me and then radiated through my womb." I close my eyes and for a moment I'm there. "Oh god," I whisper, just like I did that night.

Eric's hand comes down on my hand and he squeezes. "We don't have to do this."

"We do," I say firmly, refocusing on him. "We do." I launch back into the story. "I tried to move, but my feet were heavy, like they were planted in the ground. I looked down and blood was seeping through the skirt of my cream-colored dress. I just stared down at it as if it wasn't real, as if it was happening to someone else but then the cramps radiated through me again. I tried to get to my desk and my phone, but I couldn't. The pain was extreme, and the blood just started pouring like a faucet. It scared me and I started screaming for help."

"And Isaac came to help."

"There was no one else in the building *but* Isaac, and there's nothing between me and him. There never has been. I wasn't lying about that. I haven't lied to you." Now I'm the one squeezing his hand. "Please tell me you know that."

"I know that," he says.

My mind goes back to us outside of the Kingston building, and him pretty much telling me to go to hell before he left. "You didn't know earlier tonight."

"I *did* know," he promises. "That's why I came back. *I did know.* I told you. I let Isaac fuck with my head." He cups my face. "We would have made a beautiful baby together."

Tears well in my eyes. "We would have, wouldn't we?"

"Yes. We would have. We still could."

I blanch. "What?"

"I'm only saying, just because you lost that pregnancy doesn't mean you can't carry a baby. It wasn't our time."

"Do you want kids?"

"I didn't. I don't know, Harper. You've made me think about a lot of things in my life."

"I don't know if I even can. They said I had a problem with my uterus."

"Don't put that pressure on yourself or us. If you can't, you can't.'

"Yes, but—"

He leans in and kisses me. "If you can't, you can't. I want you, Harper. Just you. Like I have never wanted anyone." His lips close down on mine, and then his tongue does that deep sultry dance it does, and I feel each stroke everywhere. My nipples ache. My sex clenches. My entire body is humming and he's done nothing but kiss me. Some part of me knows I need to talk to him about what happened in Denver. Some part of me knows we need to talk about what he believes his brother is really doing. Some part of me knows that if someone tried to kill me tonight, they will follow me to New York City, but right now, I just want him to keep kissing me. I just want him to drug me the way he drugs me with his touch, and when he unhooks his seatbelt and mine as well, I let him pull me into his lap.

I let him turn and lower the seat and pull me down in the chair beside him, the two of us facing each other, his lips parting mine briefly, his breath fanning my cheek, my lips. "We can't do this here," I say weakly.

"I pulled the curtain, which means we're left alone," he promises even as he caresses my skirt up my legs. "And I don't have a condom," he adds. "I say we roll the dice."

"What?" I try to pull back. "But what if I get pregnant again? Eric, we just—"

He kisses me and cups my backside, pulling me against his thick erection. "Quam quae potest esse diligentissima," he murmurs next to my lips. "Another one of my tattoos that means—"

"What is meant to be," I whisper, "And I'm thankful now that my father taught me Latin."

"Yes," he replies. "What is meant to be. This is our time, Harper." And then he's kissing me again, and I have no protest in me. This is our time, but that doesn't mean that we'll end up together. What is meant to be might be the end of us, and that thought has me throwing caution to the wind. I kiss him with all that I am, like it's the last few hours we'll ever share, and I don't know why I fear that it is.

LISA RENEE JONES

CHAPTER FIVE

Eric

The past—three hours ago, right after Eric found out about the miscarriage...

My phone rings about a dozen times before it goes silent, every call from Harper. Every call ignored while I drive way too fast to be safe, as far away from her as I can get. We're done. We were done before we ever started. We were all about who could fuck who and turns out, for the time being, it's me that got fucked.

I turn down a narrow road, headed toward the private airport that is my destination, thinking Harper is just another Kingston. Princess fits her so damn well, but it doesn't seem to matter. I can't seem to shut down the storm exploding inside me. The idea of her pregnant with another man's child about kills me. The idea that Isaac has touched her when she swore he hadn't, destroys me right along with the miscarriage news. And the panic in Harper's face when I confronted her about it destroyed me, too. It *is* destroying me. *Holy fuck*, I think, I was going to be stupid and fall in love with her.

I arrive at the private airport where I've hired a jet to take me the hell out of Denver. I should have never come back. It's like I wanted to be a fool. I *am* a damn fool. I was falling in love. I let this family use her to get to me because they did. Somehow, some way, they used her to

25

get to me. I think of the bank account with the wires Harper closed. That links to Gigi and the wires we found to her account. Fucking Gigi was probably behind it all. I pull up to the private lot and kill the engine to the Jaguar. Damn straight I drive a Jag as a fuck you to the Kingstons. I should have ruined them a few months back when I had the chance, but then, it looks like they're doing a good job of it themselves. Damn though, the satisfaction of doing it now, while they fight to survive. I'm not sure Grayson can talk me out of it this time.

I kill the engine and exit the car, clicking the locks and walking into the building to the desk inside where I hand off my keys to the rep who coordinated me leasing the car. A few minutes later, I'm on a private jet, and the pilot isn't. He's running late, which is fine. I get it. I booked this flight last minute, as in really last minute, but just being on the plane takes me down ten notches, which is why I don't understand how I end up with numbers beating up my mind, pounding at me to the point that I can't think straight. I reach into my briefcase and pull out my phone and a full-sized Rubik's cube. I set my phone down and stare at it, the silence it represents bothering me more than the constant ringing. I start solving the Rubik's cube. It's done and I pull two more from my bag and repeat.

When I'm done, I have no idea why, but I pick up the phone and eye the message notifications and there are plenty of them, all from Harper. I don't understand why, but the numbers in my head want me to listen and I can't ignore them, something no one else would understand. Maybe Harper. Fuck. Where did that come from? I remind myself about the bank account. I'm going to listen to the messages and leave. The end. I punch the button the listen and Harper's voice fills the line.

"*I wanted to tell you. I just didn't want you to think I was playing you and then you got rich and I was afraid you'd think it was about money. I can't make you believe me, but you know—I'm pretty sure I'm in love with you so I just have to tell you.*" The phone beeps and disconnects. She's in love with me? What kind of game is she playing? I punch the next message.

"*I got pregnant the night we were together six years ago. I know you pulled out, but you were inside me and it happened. I wasn't with anyone else. I didn't think you'd believe me and what would forcing you to believe me achieve? It was too late to change what happened. I lost the baby.*" The machine beeps again.

I stand up. My baby? She was pregnant with *my baby?* I face the wall of the plane and press my hands to the paneling. This can't be true. This has to be a lie and yet—I push off the wall and hit the next message, sitting back down as I hear, "*When I missed my period, I thought it was stress, but then one night I was working late and suddenly I was bleeding. Lots of blood and Isaac was there and I was bad. I was hemorrhaging and—I had to let him help me. I didn't even know what was happening. I was scared and when I found out there was a baby—*" The machine beeps and I let out a guttural growl. Damn it. I hit the next message. "*Bottom line,*" she says. "*I hated so much that Isaac was the one who helped me. And I really wanted that baby, our baby, but now I'm damaged goods anyway. I don't even know now if I can have kids. They said—*"

The machine beeps and my jaw clenches. I hit the final message. "*Eric,*" she whispers. "*I didn't betray you like everyone else in this family. Have Blake hack my medical records. If I was with Isaac and he was the father, why would I fight the ER staff and insist that I couldn't be pregnant? Why wouldn't I put him down on*

27

the medical records? I just—I need you to know that I didn't betray you. You matter to me. You've always mattered to me and I regret that I didn't call you. I regret—"

There's nothing more. I inhale and take in what she just told me, numbers flying through my mind, calculating the odds of her baby being my baby. Ten percent. It's only ten percent by scientific terms, but beyond reason, I believe her. And I left her at the office, the way I left her to bleed out and suffer alone six years ago. I grab my bag, stuff the cubes back inside and start walking. It takes me ten minutes to cancel the flight and grab my rental car again.

I'm on my way back to Kingston in fifteen, dialing Adam. "Where's Harper right now?"

"At work," he says. "Why?"

"Don't let her leave. I'll be there in fifteen." I disconnect and replay the messages three times in the short drive.

I pull into the warehouse and park, dialing Adam. "I'm here. I assume she's still inside?"

"Yes. She's still inside."

"Who else is in the building?"

"They have a robot cop at the rear door who walks the place every fifteen minutes. Other than that, no one. They don't run manufacturing at night at this building."

"How do I get inside?"

"I have a hacked badge to hand off to you. Give me sixty seconds." He disconnects.

I exit my car and pocket my keys, and the minute I'm outside, a charge of unease slides down my spine. I scan the area and nothing looks off, but then, I've been ambushed by men who meant to kill me and nothing looked off. But it damn sure felt off just like now. Adam approaches me and hands me the badge. "Yes," he says, when his eyes meet mine, without me saying a word. "I feel it. I alerted our team. I have two more men on the way. They'll be here in five minutes."

"I'm going to get Harper."

"Wait until back-up is here to take her out," Adam says. "I'll call you when we're ready."

"Copy that," I say, heading for the door where I swipe my badge with success. I've just walked inside when the lights go dark. It takes me all of one second to grab my phone, light the flashlight and start running for Harper, every instinct I own telling me that she's in trouble and I can't get to her soon enough...

Present day, back in the plane...

With Harper in my chair, and the storm now past us, I kiss her like it's the last time I'll ever kiss her and with good reason. I could have lost her tonight and not just because I fucked up with her, and given her enough of a reason to kick me to the curb. Those men were in that warehouse to either scare Harper or do her harm, but I don't think it was about fear. You don't hire those kinds of pros to just scare someone. Had I not come back, I believe she'd be dead. I know it deep in my gut and that was Isaac's plan. Piss me off. Get me to leave. I fucking did it, too. I left. I not only left, I almost left her to die.

And right now, that bank account and the wires don't matter. The fact that I know that she hasn't told me everything doesn't matter. Kissing her matters. Touching her matters. I'll make her tell me everything and then the secrets won't matter anymore either.

CHAPTER SIX

Harper

I'm kissing Eric in a private airplane, in the same seat with him. Just a few hours ago, I would have believed that an impossible feat. Just days ago, I would never have believed that I'd ever see him again, let alone touch him again. He molds me closer and I press into the hard lines of his body. I don't seem to have any limits with this man. I wish I could say that I no longer have any secrets from him either, but there are things I can never say to him. They'd hurt him too badly. And I refuse to hurt him. It's a thought that has me kissing him harder, deeper. I want to just get lost in this man and I know that's not even possible. Someone tried to kill me tonight.

"Wait," I pant, pressing on his chest. "No. I'm forgetting what happened. I'm forgetting what we just ran from. You say out of sight, out of mind. You say they'll let me go, but what if they won't? What if they, whoever they are, follow me? We don't know what this is about. We don't know what they want. What if I bring the problems to you? What if I'm the reason your real life is shaken up or rocked? Destroyed even."

"My real life?" he queries. "Sweetheart, you are my real life."

"You have a fortune and career and friends in New York City. I don't think I can go there with you until we know what this is. I can't. We have to turn around or redirect. I can pick a city and just go stay there. Even someplace in New York. I just need to know that I won't cause you problems."

He rolls me slightly to my back, as much as the seat allows. "You do know I was trying to fuck you thirty thousand feet in the air, right?"

"Fuck me thirty thousand feet in the air after you tell me that I'm not going to put you, or people you care about, in danger."

"The people I care about—Grayson and his future wife—they heard I was worried about you, and immediately wanted me to send you to them to protect."

"They did? They don't even know me."

"Grayson knows all about you, Harper. You know that. You saw that when you showed up at the office."

"Yes," I whisper, "and I was shocked. I didn't—"

"Think you impacted me like you did?"

"Exactly. I didn't."

"Well, you did, and for the record, I didn't think the princess gave the bastard two shits of a thought after I left."

"You know better."

"Now," he says. "But bottom line, we let time pass that didn't have to pass. That night we began might not have been our time, but it could have come sooner. You belong with me now. We do this together."

Together. I belong with him. Those words do all kinds of wonderful things to every part of me, inside and out. I want to believe they're true. I want to believe no one can ruin this for us, but I know that there is much at hand at present. Too much, I fear. "Together means that we protect the people we care about."

"No one I care about will be in danger by us going to New York," he assures me. "I wouldn't let that happen.

Just like I wasn't leaving you back there. I won't ever leave you there again."

The implications of his words are broad and I don't want to let myself go where they lead. Not with this much drama, not with the risks this family represents to the rest of his life.

"Whatever you're thinking," he says, squeezing my knee, "stop. You said a lot of things on those messages, things I understand. Things we're going to talk about when you're in my bed, in my home, where I'll make sure you feel safe." My cheeks heat. I told him I might love him. I know that's what he's talking about. "You want to take it back now?" he challenges.

I swallow hard and meet his stare. "No, I don't, but what happened to us talking about this in your apartment? I thought you said we were—"

"We are," he says, his voice low, rough, and he leans over me. "God, woman, you have no idea how much hearing those voicemails affected me. You no idea how much you scared me tonight."

"I was never with Isaac."

"I'm not talking about Isaac. I'm talking about those men in the warehouse. Fuck." He rests his forehead against mine. "I couldn't get to you fast enough."

"But you did. When I needed you, you were there and you have no idea how much that means to me."

"I left," he says, his voice turning gravelly. "I left, and if I hadn't come back, I don't want to think about what would've happened."

"You came back," I say, barely able to breathe now. "Both times I needed you, you showed up."

"Because I can't stay away, not from you. From the rest of that family, yes, but not you."

"Then don't," I order, pushing on his chest and forcing his gaze to mine. "Don't stay away. Don't go away. Just don't."

I've barely spoken the words before his lips are on my lips. His mouth closes over mine, and I can taste his urgency, his fear. Fear I recognize as my own. I'd been certain that after he'd learned about the miscarriage we'd never be here like this again. I press into the hard lines of his body, drinking in his passion, consumed, so very willingly consumed, all that he is and could be to me. A dark feeling, a sensation that I know started back at the warehouse, even before the lights went out, tries to surface, and I try to shove it away.

Desperate to escape all those pained feelings I felt when he left, when he refused to listen to me, I lose myself in the moment. I lose myself in Eric and I tumble deeper into passion, heat low in my belly, desire spreading slick and hot between my thighs.

For now, forever if I had my way, there's nothing but the stroke of Eric's tongue, the spicy male scent of him, the demanding taste of him. His hands on my body, under my backside, molding me possessively to his body. God, how I need this man. I can't get enough.

I tug at his shirt, but the space is too small for me to free it from his pants. Instead, my palms caress the flex of his hard body beneath his clothes. He responds to my desperation, a low, gruff sound of hunger rumbling in his chest that I revel in. I want him to want me. I want him to feel the same pleasure I feel with his touch when I touch him. He squeezes my backside again and I can feel the thick ridge of his erection against my belly when I want him inside me.

His hand slides up my skirt, over my thigh and there is something about this man's touch that can be gentle and rough in the same moment, and I like it. "Harper," he whispers, his lips traveling my jaw, down to my neck, distracting me for a brief moment before his fingers are under my panties, stroking that wet heat that drenches me and now his fingers. I pant with the flick of my clit, and then he's pressing inside me—one finger, two, his mouth closing over mine, tongue licking my tongue, even as he does wicked things to my body.

I grab his arm, fingers closing around his shirt, sensations rocking my body, and I can't stop what comes next. His thumb is working just the right spot while his fingers pump all the right places, and I am in that perfect place, where you both want to come and want to hold back, but I can't. I tumble into a shuddering, quaking, incredible release, and when my body collapses in sated satisfaction, Eric leans in, his lips at my ear. "I'm learning your sweet spots. Soon I'll know everything. I'll know all of your secrets."

Those words are not an accident.

He's telling me he believes that I am still keeping secrets. And I am, but not the kind he wants to know. Not the kind he *needs* to know and I have to be strong enough not to tell him. Not to hurt him the way my secrets—no, not my secrets, my knowledge of past history, of *his* history—would hurt him.

CHAPTER SEVEN

Harper

In every lie there is the truth.

With Eric, I want to be all about the truth, especially considering all the lies Isaac made him believe tonight. I don't want to hurt him, but as I lie here with him on the plane, with his whisper about secrets in my ear, it's killing me to believe I know things he doesn't know.

Eric kisses my temple. "I need to log onto the internet and get an update."

It's the kiss on my temple that undoes me. He wants to trust me. He proved that by coming back for me tonight. I want to deserve that trust. I *do* deserve it. The only secret I had that was mine, he now knows. The rest is history that serves no purpose besides hurting him and eating me alive. Okay, maybe I do have a secret. No, it's more of a gray area where I didn't tell him everything, but I didn't lie. It just wasn't necessary that he know the rest of the story. And that story matters zero in present day.

Zero.

It serves no purpose but to hurt him, I repeat in my mind, because my guilt could easily make me selfish. Clearly, my clear conscience would make me feel better but at his expense.

He shifts and the recliner lifts. When I would get up and move, he actually moves with me and we end up at a half-moon-shaped booth. I slide into the seat and he walks away to grab a briefcase. It's then that I jolt with realization. "I have nothing with me," I say as Eric joins me. "And I'm not talking about clothes. My phone and computer and all my work. Eric, anything I'd researched and found they'll find. Whoever they are—Isaac, I assume."

"Isaac's involved," he confirms, sitting down next to me. "Of that, there's no doubt, but I'm guessing my father is as well." He scoots close to me and removes a MacBook from the briefcase. "I left my things in my rental as well. This is Walker equipment. They wanted us to have a way to communicate with them on the ground." He keys up the screen.

I have no idea how they communicated all this information, but then again, it doesn't matter. We're safe. We have support. We have a way to communicate with the ground. He keys the Mac to life and the magnitude of our situation, and what happened to me earlier, rushes over me.

"Thank you, Eric," I breathe out, flashing back to that dark warehouse. Then to his proclamation of fear over everything that could have happened to me tonight. "Thank you for coming back."

His expression is all dark shadows, his eyes full of torment. Torment that I know he shows few people, if anyone, but he lets me see the emotions in him now. It matters. It shows me he's here with me, that he's willing to let me see the real man and the savant beneath his walls of armor.

The air shifts around us and then this swell of heat and intensity blossoms, consuming us. I can't breathe when he's this close and yet I can't imagine ever breathing again if he left.

"I wasn't okay when you left," I whisper, not sure why I make the confession. "Not even close to okay. I can't fall for you, Eric, and have you leave. You have to talk to me. You have to give me a chance to explain what you don't understand."

The MacBook beeps with a message and he ignores it, sliding a hand under my hair to settle on my neck. "I'm not leaving, Harper." My hand lands on his chest, and his heart races under my palm. Or maybe it's my heart racing, radiating through my palm into his chest. I don't know where I start and end with this man. There is just what I was before him and what I am with him.

"I told you," he adds. "We're together now."

"You said that before you left." I pull back and look at him. "You *did* leave. I'm so very thankful that you came back and not just because of that warehouse. You heard the voicemails. You know what state I was in before the warehouse went dark. I was destroyed when you left and I don't even know what to do with that. No other human being has ever had that power over me."

"I was no better." He shuts his eyes and seems to struggle before he looks at me. "I had things pounding at my mind."

"Things? Numbers?"

"Yes. Yes, Harper. No one does that to me anymore, and I have to want you really damn badly to let you know you can do that to me. It's a weakness. I don't like weaknesses."

"I'm a weakness?" That cuts and I try to pull away.

He holds onto me. "Caring about someone is a weakness," he says, echoing my thoughts from moments before. "It opens you up to pain and hurt. We just choose to make it worth the risk. And you are."

I understand what he's saying. Losing my dad tore me to pieces. Fear for my mother drives me daily, but there is more to the confessions now between us. "I wish I didn't know that I could trigger the savant in a bad way.

I don't want to be a trigger like that. I want to be someone who calms you. I want—"

He leans in and kisses me, a deep slide of tongue before he says, "You can be. In time, you can be that for me. With trust, there are many things we can be together, Harper."

It's then that I know I have to tell him what I've held back. I have to tell him all the shitty ways this family has tried to hurt him, and be done with it. At least then, despite the pain it will cause, it won't be pain *I* caused, and I now think that's a critical part of us moving forward. "Eric—"

The messages on the MacBook explode with back-to-back beeps and he kisses me. "Hold that thought. I need to see what the hell is going on." He turns away to read the messages and I'm suddenly alarmed. We're in the air. My mother is on the ground. What if something goes wrong?

"What's happening?" I ask, scooting closer and trying to see over his shoulder. "Is everyone safe?"

"Yes," he says, typing a reply before he glances at me. "My father and Isaac showed up at the warehouse and apparently had a blow up in front of the building."

"Because I'm still alive? Or because your father found out Isaac tried to kill me and went nuts?"

He stops mid-sentence of whatever he's typing and turns to me. "Maybe the latter. I don't know." His expression says nothing more but it's there, in the air.

"What do you and Blake think?"

"Undecided. On one side, I don't like the way they tried to get me out of the picture before tonight happened. That seems like they wanted to end you, and they knew I wouldn't let that happen. On the other side, if you ended up dead, they had to believe that I'd come back for revenge. Then again, I let them get away with hurting my mother." He cuts his stare.

"You were a teenager." I grab his arm. "You were a kid and you followed her wishes."

He looks at me. "What are your wishes, Harper?"

It feels like a test. Like his need to hear that my loyalty is to him, not them. I don't know how he can question this, but I get it. I'm still the princess until I prove I'm right here with him, all the way until the end. "I don't want to take any shit from them ever again. Hurt them if they deserve it."

"They deserved it before I ever met you."

"Don't hold back for me. Ever."

His eyes glint with something I don't quite understand. "Are you sure about that?" he asks softly.

"Yes. I'm sure."

"Then now is the time when I ask you a question before I assume the answer. I ask. You answer. Tell me the truth."

Unease slides through me. I don't know what this is about. I don't know at all, but I dive head first into the uncharted waters. "I will. Ask. Whatever it is, I'll answer honestly."

"Why did Kingston wire large sums of money into an account in your name that you later closed?"

Suddenly, I feel as if the floor of the plane is opening up and sucking me into the turbulence.

CHAPTER EIGHT

Harper

My hand is at my throat as I turn away from Eric, trying to calm down. A bank account in my name, with wire transfers, which is now closed. I'm still trying to recover from this fact when Eric pushes forward. "Talk to me, Harper," Eric says. "Be honest, no matter how bad it is."

My gaze rockets to his. "I have two accounts. Checking and savings. I've had the savings since I was ten. I've had the checking since I moved to Denver years ago. I don't have, nor have I *ever* had any account that received wires. I also haven't closed an account."

He studies me, his expression impassive, unreadable, his blue eyes steely, his jaw hard.

"I promise you, Eric. I promise on my mother's life. I swear to God above. I'm telling you the truth."

He turns away from me, keys into the MacBook and then stares at the screen for a few beats before turning it for me to look at what appears to be my bank account. I grab the MacBook and study the account, and my God. It looks like it's mine. I check the data, all that I can see online, and it's a terrifying match for me. I then scan the wires and the sum of money that came into this account and what's left is six figures many times over. My stomach rolls.

"I need a bathroom," I say, sliding out of the booth and hurrying down the small walkway toward what I think is my destination. When I find the small alcove, I grab the door there and enter a space that is as compact as most airlines, despite this being a private plane. I shut the door and I do what anyone would in here. I go to the bathroom. I wash my hands. I act like normal activity will make this go away right up until the point that the normal activity is over. Now I'm just standing in a tiny space, staring at myself in the mirror. How have I given this much of myself to this family to end up here?

Eric knocks on the door. "Harper. Open up."

Open up and say what?

To him, I'm a liar. Again. Anger surges in me and I yank the door open to find him big and intimidatingly male, filling the doorway and the entire exterior space. It doesn't make me back down. "I thought you wanted to talk about the miscarriage, but obviously, you didn't get me up here, trapped in a cage, to talk about a baby that meant nothing to you. You brought me up here to corner me about a bank account that isn't even mine. You don't want to trust me. You want to prove I'm the damn princess you can hate. You wanted me to be her so badly that you carved her name on your body." I shove against him. "Move. I need to get out of here."

He shackles my wrists and in a quick second, I'm against the wall next to the door, and he's all but suffocating me with muscle and man. "Don't bully me. I don't like it."

"You think the baby we lost means nothing to me? Are you fucking serious?"

"Yes, I am. You never said it mattered to you."

"Again I ask, *are you fucking serious*?"

"Did it?"

"Yes. It did." He cuts his gaze, turbulence flooding off of him before his jaw sets harder and he pins me in an arrow of a stare. "You're deflecting."

"Like you did with the baby?"

"You're pushing me in ways you don't want to push me, Harper."

"Or what? What are you going to do? Kill me for them?"

His eyes glint hard, anger burning deep and dark before he releases me and starts walking away.

Shocked, I sink down against the wall and I swear my knees go weak. Right when I feel as if the floor of the plane is opening up to suck me out again, Eric is back, pulling me to him. "I would have wanted to know and father our child. I would have loved our child. You matter to me. Everything you said in those messages matters to me, but I want us to talk about those things when we land because I want us to be on the same page when we get to New York. Me and you against the world. Meet me halfway, Harper."

"It's not my account. I swear, Eric, it's not mine." My fingers curl around his shirt. "It's not mine, but how are you going to believe me? How can you ever believe me?"

He studies me all of two seconds. "I believe you."

I blanch. "What?"

"I'd know if you were lying. I'd see it in your eyes." He leans in and brushes his lips over mine, a soft, lingering touch before he whispers, "I'd taste it on your lips." He pulls back. "We'll handle this. Together."

"How do we handle it? How does this even happen? How can anyone open an account in my name?"

"There are hackers like Blake Walker who have the skills to do it." The messages on his MacBook beep in rapid succession and he kisses my hand. "Come on. Let's sit and make sure we end this."

I don't know what that means, but he's already walking and taking me with him. We settle back into the booth and he is immediately exchanging messages with whoever is on iMessage. "A Walker team member followed one of the men from the warehouse. He's tailing him now. No word on who he is yet." He sends another message, followed by another and then turns to me. "Blake is going to make the bank account history disappear. By the time we're on the ground, it won't exist."

"Just like that?"

"He's one of the best hackers on planet earth," he says. "So no, not just like that. Just like Blake. We're damn lucky to have him working with us."

"Do you know what those wires were used for?"

"Not yet. Blake's going to have us go to their facility when we arrive and we're going to talk all of this through, which is why we're going to need to get some sleep." He shuts his MacBook and when he would stand up again, I catch his arm.

"I'm being framed, right?"

"Or just used. We can't know for sure. That's what we'll work with Blake and his team to figure out." He kisses me. "Come on. Let's lie down. We need to be alert when we land and we only have about three hours to sleep." He moves away and stands. I let him help me to my feet, but I'm not naïve. He's trying to avoid something but even before we talk about what I feel it might be, I need to say something else to him.

He guides us to two side by side lounge recliners and we sit down. I turn to him. "I'm sorry. I was all over the place by the bathroom and—"

He kisses me with his hand on my head, his tongue stroking deep, the taste of him drugging before he says, "It's been an emotional night that will eventually end

46

with you in my bed. I'll deal with everything in between to get you there." He caresses my cheek and hits a button that starts to lower my seat before doing the same of his.

A minute later, we're on our sides, facing each other, the intimacy between us a bubble of warmth I want to live inside, get lost inside, but I can't yet. Not until I process the implications of that bank account that keep hitting me from all sides. "If they framed me with that bank account, and who knows what else, maybe when you showed up they got spooked. Maybe that's why those men came at me. Maybe I was a get out of jail free card. If I died and I was framed for whatever this is, this ends." Another thought hits me and I sit up straight. "Oh God." I turn to Eric. "Oh God." I raise my seat and he follows. I stand up because I can't sit. I can't stand the idea in my head.

Eric follows me to the aisle and turns me to face him. "What is it?"

"What if Gigi sent me to get you so she could frame you for my murder in some way?"

CHAPTER NINE

Eric

What if Gigi used her to set me up and frame me for her murder?

The plane starts to quake around us again. Harper and I still stand in the middle of the aisle, almost as if the damn universe is answering her fears, telling us that yes, Gigi plotted Harper's murder, and in turn, my blame for her death.

Death.

Harper's murder.

Just the idea of finding her to lose her again guts me.

"Eric?" Harper presses when I haven't replied. "You aren't saying anything. You think I'm right, don't you?"

The plane quakes again, this time violently. I catch the ceiling, and mold Harper close, holding onto her, the way I plan to hold onto her from this point forward. I can't explain how she's become that important to me, but she has. I think she's been a part of me since I met her, I just didn't want to admit it. Not when, in my mind, she was one of them.

"Let's sit back down," I say. "We need to buckle up."

"Do you think Gigi—"

The plane drops and I have to grab the damn seat to keep us from tumbling. The minute I have stable ground, if you can call anything about where we're at right now stable, I rotate us and plant Harper in her seat. Another

49

rumbling of the plane beneath my feet has my hands planting on the arms of her chair. "Eric," she breathes out, grabbing my shirt as if she's trying to protect me, not steady herself. Like she could hold onto me and keep me from flying if we jolted much more. "I won't let them use me to get to you."

She says those words with such passion and emotion that I wonder how I ever doubted her, but I know. *They* are why I doubted her. I let them get into my head and I judged her the same way they judged me: by where she came from. "They don't get to use either of us anymore, Harper. No more." The plane calms for a moment and I buckle her seatbelt. "We'll win. I promise you." I sit down and secure myself in my seat.

She turns to me and gives me a turbulent look. "Do you think Gigi—" she begins again, but I cut her off.

"All I can confirm, and all I know right now, is that I wouldn't be surprised if Gigi popped champagne when my mother killed herself."

"You really think they were trying to kill me tonight, don't you?"

I stroke her hair. "Sweetheart, I've got you. I *will* protect you."

"That's a yes."

"That's a 'we won't rule out any possibility.'"

"What happens when they come for me in New York City?"

"They won't be that foolish," I assure her, and I believe that to be true. "They know I'll be waiting. They know I'll be ready, especially after tonight."

"If they believe I'm the way to cover up whatever you're about to discover, they might be desperate."

"That bank account was wiped out," I remind her. "They can't pin anything on you."

"We have no idea what else they might have on me, what else they framed me for."

"We knew about the bank account," I counter. "And anything else digital Blake has found."

"There could be paper trails, things I did that I didn't know I was doing. Eric, that meeting with the union I was supposed to have—it felt weird. It felt like a set-up. I actually thought that when I found out about it."

"What kind of set-up?"

"At the time, I thought they were going to make it look like I screwed things up with the union to fire me. A way to get rid of me for bringing you here. Now, I'm not so sure, Eric. Maybe it was something more nefarious. Who knows what kind of ways they've been setting me up to be a fall guy. After tonight, I'm afraid I've been blind and stupid."

"No," I say. "You're not blind. You're not stupid. You had a gut feeling about the union meeting. When we get to New York City, we'll sit down and tune into any instinct you had that might guide us. Sleep now. We only have a couple of hours until we land and we'll plan this out."

"How can I sleep? The plane. This damn family. My mother back there with them."

"Your mother is safe."

"Can we warn Walker Security that Gigi might be involved? What if me leaving has them turn on her?"

"You know Walker is already watching her. They're damn good. They've thought of everything we've thought of."

"How can you be sure? If this was your mother—"

"You're right," I say. "You're absolutely right." The plane is calm enough, for the moment at least, that I unbuckle and walk to the table where I left the MacBook in a compartment under the wooden top. I grab it, hold on as we shake a good thirty seconds and then make my way back to my seat. Once I'm secure again, I pull up the MacBook and try to connect but this time it's a no-go. I show Harper the message I'm getting. "Sorry, sweetheart. It's just not going to happen." I shove the Mac into a pocket by my chair and turn to Harper. "Adam's in charge in Denver and he's damn good. He'll protect your mother with his life. I promise you this. Rest, princess."

"Princess?"

"I like that name for you," I say, my voice rasping with about ten emotions I can't name. "You're *my princess*, not theirs. Not ever again. They don't get to define us, remember?"

"But you—"

I lean in and kiss her. "Want you like I have never wanted in my life. Now rest. You won't get to rest when you're in my bed. Not the first night. Hell, maybe not the first month."

A faint smile touches her lips but doesn't quite reach her eyes. I want it to reach her eyes and that means ending the Kingston hell she's in. Fuck. I should have ended the Kingstons when I wanted to end them. When I was five seconds from doing it, and doing it with proverbial dynamite. I lean her seat back and stand up to grab the blanket and pull it over her. I then crank my seat back as well and face her.

I cup her face and my thumb strokes her cheek. "Shut your eyes and think of something that makes you happy."

"Ending this would make me happy."

"Then I'll end it, just to make you happy."

She gives me another half smile. "Just to make me happy?"

"Yes, princess. Just to make you happy."

Her hand settles on my princess tattoo. "Maybe princess isn't such a bad nickname. Not when you say it like you just did."

"How did I just say it?"

"All low and rough and sexy."

"Sexy, huh?"

"Yes," she whispers. "Everything about you is sexy." Her cheeks don't heat this time. She's not flirting. She's just being raw and real, and fuck, I need raw and real. I need *her*.

"Show me," I reply softly, "when we get to my bed. Sleep now, while the plane seems to have calmed again."

Her lashes lower and seconds pass before she whispers, "I can't believe you really came back."

I'm going to change that, I think. I'm going to make sure she knows that I won't just come back. I won't leave. Ever. I lay there and watch her for a good thirty minutes until I'm certain she's asleep. Then and only then, do I grab the MacBook and try Walker again. This time I connect and Blake goes live immediately.

Anything new? I type.

He replies with: *Nothing urgent enough to discuss while you're in the air. Everyone is safe and secure. We're gathering data to review with you when you arrive. Anything I need to know or relay to Adam?*

I type: *We suspect Harper is being set-up as a fall guy who ended up too dead to defend herself.*

His reply: *My thoughts as well.*

And I add, responding immediately: *We have reason to believe Gigi played a role in helping set me up for her murder. With Harper now under our protection, we need to be sure Gigi and the family don't turn on Harper's mother. Keep Gigi away from her.*

He doesn't reply immediately. Seconds tick by and I push for a response: *Blake?*

Another twenty seconds pass, each one grinding along my nerve endings, and he finally answers: *Harper's mother is at Gigi's house. I'm sending Adam in as a maintenance man to check on her.*

I look at Harper, her skin pale perfection, features beautiful in rest and trust. She trusted me to take care of her and her mother or she wouldn't be asleep. My jaw sets hard and I type a message to Blake: *Get her mother out of there and I don't care how you do it. Adam needs to throw her over his damn shoulder if that's what it takes.*

CHAPTER TEN

Eric

The internet goes dark again about two hours before we land, which forces me to do what I need to do anyway. I manage to settle into my seat and sleep with one thought in mind: hell waits for us when we get to the ground. I need to be mentally and physically ready. I wake before Harper and for a moment I lay there facing her in my chair, and fuck, I just stare at her. She's beautiful. She's mine even if she doesn't know it yet. Mine to protect. A thought that has me sitting up and checking for an internet connection again with no success. I store my MacBook back in the pocket and lay back down, reaching out to caress Harper's cheek, her lashes dark half moons on her perfect skin. She doesn't wake up. Right now, she's with me, in the air, safe, and some part of her knows that.

Some part of her trusts me the way I told her I need to trust her. The problem is that I'm a fucking hypocrite. I've demanded honesty from her but I haven't told her everything. I have my own secrets. Things I'll have to share with her once I know she knows me. Once I know she can read past the history I've drawn to see me now. I need to build trust and damn it, that means keeping my promise to keep her mother safe, but I'm not on the ground. Adam is. I'm trusting Adam to keep my promise to Harper.

Adam is the one protecting her mother.

Adam

Denver, CO

A master of disguise.

It's what I do, a skill I learned while on the road with my mother and her boyfriend, along with their pack of criminal friends during most of my youth. I'm dressed as a repairman in a blue jumpsuit with a pair of brown contacts over my blue eyes. My black hair is slicked back. I ring the bell of the stucco home wrapped in ivy and wait for an answer.

A young brunette housekeeper answers the door. "Yes?"

"There's a gas leak." I show her a clipboard. "We need to check the lines running in and out of the house to assure we aren't on the verge of a catastrophic event."

"Oh God," the woman says. "That sounds bad."

"I'll need access inside to determine where the pipes run but from what I can tell from the maps, it's along the line of your kitchen and the backyard."

"I need to get this approved. Do you have a number I can just confirm this by calling?"

I shove a card at her that will ring to Blake. "Call. Make it fast. Time is critical."

She grabs her phone from her pocket and dials the number on the official-looking card complete with the gas company's address and logo. She speaks to Blake and her eyes go wide. A moment later, she disconnects. "Come in, please." She backs up and allows me to enter the house.

I walk inside, finding myself in the center of a towering foyer with a fancy chandelier above my head that would make a good weapon, should one need one. It might not be how most people think of fancy lighting, but it works for me. I follow the woman, who hasn't introduced herself or asked for my name, through an archway to find an open-concept living room with expensive, Regency-style furnishings that scream "grandma."

The woman who I know to be Celia Rodriquez, the housekeeper of five years, motions toward a doorway that leads to a closed kitchen. "I'll need to step outside as well."

"There's a door off the kitchen."

I nod and head for the kitchen, aware of Celia's need to leave to pick up her kids. She hurries down a hallway, which means she'll be updating Gigi on my presence. She's headed toward what our blueprints show to be an office. I walk into the kitchen, set down my toolbox and crack the kitchen door to the backyard to find my job just got easier. Not only is a fire crackling in a massive stone fireplace, but Gigi and Danielle, Harper's mother, are standing in front of it while Celia, who clearly tracked them down via the office patio door, tells them about my presence.

The chat with Celia is short and she departs, which means she'll be coming back here in about five minutes. "Answer me, Gigi," Danielle demands. "Did you really help convince Eric to come here?"

"I didn't convince him," Gigi snaps. "He hates me. Harper convinced him to come here. Your daughter knows we need help even if you don't."

"We don't need help," Danielle says.

Gigi laughs. "Are you playing dumb or are you really that stupid?"

"My daughter is smitten with him. He's rich and good looking."

"Like my son that you married? Sounds like you're two of a kind. Mother and daughter."

"Stop being a bitch," Danielle snaps. "Stop. I love your son. I'm protecting him, and bringing Eric here doesn't protect him."

"You seem very afraid of Eric. Why is that?"

"Your son doesn't want Eric here."

"Eric is my son's child. He's my grandchild."

"Eric's our enemy."

"Seems to me none of us know who our real enemies are, now do we?"

"Why does that feel like a threat?" Danielle quips back.

"Why do you see threats that no one else sees? But you want a threat," Gigi adds. "I might be old, but I protect what's mine. Everything you think is yours has always been mine."

Footsteps sound behind me and I shut the sliding door to face Celia. "All clear in here. I was about to head outside." I don't wait on her to reply. I reach for the door again, only to have it open as Danielle, an older version of Harper, runs smack into me.

"I'm so sorry," she says. "I'm—" She blinks up at me. "I just need to get by."

I step back as she swipes at her cheek, as if hiding tears, and then darts away. I hit a button on my phone that sends a message to my man outside the house. He'll follow Danielle. I'm here. I'm going to listen in and find out what Gigi does next.

I turn to look at Celia. "I'll be fast."

She nods. "I'll be back in a minute to check on you." She quickly follows Danielle.

I take the freedom and exit to the backyard and Gigi has her back to me, and thanks to poor hearing, she doesn't know I'm here. She sits in a chair by the fire and makes a call. "I need to speak to you," she says. "Where are you? Why aren't you answering my calls?"

She disconnects and just sits there. And continues to sit there as if she knows whoever she called will call her back. I need to know who she called. I enter the kitchen, shut the door, and text Blake: *Who did Gigi just call?*

His answer is instant: *Kingston Senior.*

I frown. Kingston Senior is supposed to be pissed that Eric was brought into this. Why did Gigi just call him like the two of them have a secret? Like they're working a plan? Are mother and son behind the attack on Harper and the set-up of Eric for the murder?

Fuck.

Are mother and son really moving on to kill Harper's mother in her place?

I start walking. I need Danielle in my sights and I need her in my sights now. If she dies, it's on me.

Eric

We're about to touch down and incredibly, Harper has yet to move. "Wake up, princess." I stroke her hair. "We're landing."

Her eyes go wide and she tries to sit up, but she gets caught in the seatbelt. "Any news?" She frees herself. "Is my mother okay?"

"No news," I say, wishing like hell that wasn't the truth. I hit the button to raise her seat. "The internet has been out for the past few hours."

"Hours? It's been hours?" She runs her hand through her hair. "I need to know she's okay. I can't believe I even slept."

"Your mother is fine. We have eyes on her with Walker Security. And you slept, because you were exhausted, with good reason. It's not been an easy twenty-four hours."

"Did you sleep? Please tell me you did. I don't even remember us laying down to rest."

"I did," I say, amazed at how she worries about me. No one worries about me. I don't let them close enough to even think about me. The engines shift for landing and I glance at my watch and then back at Harper. "It's one in the morning. We'll make it to Blake's offices before sunrise, talk with him for a few hours, and then go try to get some more rest." We hit the runway and I grab Harper's hand, lacing our fingers together. "In my bed, Harper. Together. Something to look forward to."

"Hmm. Yes." Her eyes light. "It is. I want to see how the bastard lives. I wonder what your bedroom looks like. Do you secretly have a fetish for pink?"

"The only fetish I have is you," I assure her, pleased that she's, at least momentarily, forgotten the danger on the ground.

"And that," I add, "is no secret." My phone buzzes with a text, signaling we're now at tower level. I grab my cell and glance down at the screen to find a message from Adam that reads: *Call me.*

I dial his number and he answers in one ring with, "About damn time."

A reply that sets me on edge, or rather, more on edge than I already am. "We're still in the air. Talk to me."

Harper grabs my arm. "Is that Adam? Is my mother safe?"

"Is Danielle safe?" I ask, relaying her worry.

"Yes," Adam says. "Danielle's safe."

I glance at Harper and give a nod. She breathes out in relief and settles into her seat.

"But there's an interesting twist," Adam adds.

"I'm listening," I say, choosing my words cautiously as to not alarm Harper.

"Danielle fought with Gigi. Gigi then called your father and I got the impression it might be the two of them plotting against you and Harper. He never returned her call, but he did something far more interesting. He got on a plane to New York City. Your father is on his way to you and Harper."

What the hell? I think, biting back the words, again, for Harper's benefit.

"What else?"

"Private plane. I'll let you know when he's on the ground. It's a couple hours behind you."

We exchange a few more coded words and disconnect.

"What's happening?" Harper asks, leaning in close. "What just happened because I can tell you were choosing your words cautiously and that makes me nervous all over again."

More like, what the hell *is happening?* I think as the numbers in my mind start to spin, looking for my father's angle, and one word keeps coming to me over and over, wanting to be recognized: Murder. There is murder in the air and I need to keep Harper close and safe.

LISA RENEE JONES

CHAPTER ELEVEN

Harper

My relief over hearing my mother is safe is short-lived. I didn't miss the way Eric disconnected his call without looking at me or the subtle, but distinct, stiffening of his spine. My mother might be safe, but something's wrong. "Eric." I touch his arm. "Talk to me."

Seconds tick by before he looks at me, his blue eyes unreadable, hard. "Your mother is safe," he repeats, tension vibrating off of him.

"I know that," I say, reminded of what he said about triggers that create a paralyzing influx of numbers in his mind. Whatever is wrong isn't about my mother. It's about him.

My hand goes to his hand, and I turn it over, pressing our palms together but I don't push him to talk. He doesn't look at me, his lashes lowering, his expression tightening. I wait, silently letting him know that I'm here, until finally, his eyes open. "My father's on his way to New York City."

It's an odd development, unexpected even, but what strikes me now is Eric's mood, his edginess. This man is an ex-SEAL and a billionaire savant, who has taken on enemies and the world and this family, even his father, yet right now, his father hangs in the air between us like a nuclear bomb about to drop and blow holes in him.

I search his handsome face that is all hard lines and shadows, his expression unreadable. "Why is he coming to New York City?"

"Why do you think he's coming?"

"I don't know," I say. "You tell me."

"To fuck with me, Harper." He's intense. He's big-time intense.

"I know that we're new," I say. "I know that I haven't spent every day of the last six years with you, but I've experienced your reactions to your father to some degree, and it's not like this. What else is going on?"

He cuts his stare, unhooks his seatbelt and his hands flatten on his knees. "I need out of this plane," he says, and I have this sense he's coming out of his own skin or perhaps drowning in a sea of numbers.

The exterior doors to the plane open and I'm confused, not sure what to do next, aside from just trying to be here with him, the way he decided to be here for me when he followed me back to Denver. I lean over and kiss his cheek and when I pull back, there's surprise in his eyes I really don't understand. A moment later, his hand is cupping my head and he's kissing me deeply and fiercely, before he says, "And I need *you*."

He speaks those words with a deep raspy voice that I feel like a vibration through my body. He needs me. I never thought I'd hear those words from this man. "I need you, too."

The minute I speak those words, the tension in his body eases, his expression softens. "Show me when we're finally alone. Come on. Let's get out." He stands and helps me to my feet, and my instinct is to reach for the jacket I don't have with me. I have nothing of my own at all. No coat. No purse. No phone. I've left everything in Denver, including my mother.

Eric urges me into the aisle and I point at the MacBook. "Do you need that?"

"Walker will come pick it up."

"What about your rental car? And my car is still at the office, though I don't think that's an issue."

"Walker will take care of it for you. I talked to Adam about my rental and your car before we took off."

"I didn't give them my keys."

"They'll figure it out."

He means dig in my purse, which feels invasive, but at this point, I think I just need to be glad to be here and safe.

Eric's hand slides to my back, urging me forward ahead of him, but I rotate to face him instead. "Thank you for saving me, Eric," I say, my hand flattening on his chest, "I'll l fight for you just as hard as you've proven you'll fight for me."

His eyes soften, warm, a gentler side of Eric surfacing, and I feel the connection between us like a blast of warm sun on a cold day.

"You tried to shoot my attacker, Harper. I know you will. Come on. Let's get out of this pile of steel you were certain was going to kill us."

"Don't go there," I say, letting him turn me toward the door, before I glance over my shoulder and add, "We shouldn't have been in the air."

We joke back and forth about that decision, and while yes, Eric is fully engaged in the exchange, I can still feel the tension in him, no doubt, the aftermath of hearing his father is coming here. My bond with my father was special. His bond with his father is poison, even more so than I'd ever imagined.

We exit side by side and travel the narrow, double-wide stairs into the dark, cold night. I block out the weather as best I can without a coat and manage to glance at Eric's watch; it's eleven in Denver, which makes it's one in the morning here. A really cold early morning, I decide, as we hit the runway and a gust of New York wind that is ten times colder than the Denver chill I know well. It's damp and biting in a way the low altitude makes possible, but the truth is, Denver is cold and biting beyond the weather. In this moment, I know that I've allowed it to be my prison, that I've allowed the beauty of the city and the beauty of the family I once knew in my father and mother, to seduce me, to hold onto me. I didn't want to let go of what I'd lost in my father, so I held onto what I had left of him. The wind gusts again and Eric throws his arm around me, pulling me close.

"That's our ride," Eric says, as an SUV halts a few feet in front of us.

By the time we're at the vehicle, a big brute of a man meets us at the rear door and holds it open. "Savage," Eric greets as I climb into the back of the vehicle. "Good to see you, man." An easy greeting that speaks of trust, and right about now, trust is good.

The two men talk for a full minute, their voices muffled, before Eric joins me inside, and Savage shuts the door behind him. "We're going straight to my apartment after all," Eric announces.

"I thought we were going to the Walker offices?"

"They're coming to us. It's more secure that way." Alarm bells go off in my head but before I can ask what exactly that means—aren't we safe here?—he's already moving on. "Grayson's wife, Mia, took the liberty of grabbing you a few necessities. They're stopping by as well."

I forget about the security issues as they relate to me and focus on his friends. "Should they do that? I mean someone, three someones, attacked me tonight.

Professionals even, you said. What if coming near me, and us, puts them in danger?"

"Before I heard my father was headed this direction I thought we were safe here. That's why I was considering sending you to Grayson, to keep you safe."

"And now?"

"Now, the jury's out, but Grayson already knows what's going on. He won't stay away. If I'm in trouble, he's in trouble. That's how we operate."

Friends. That word is hollow to me. I have no friends. My life has been this family and therefore it's empty.

"The harder I push Grayson away," Eric continues, "the closer he'll step, which is why I need to see him now, today, and convince him all is well."

"So he'll step back."

"Yes. So he'll step back and we need him to step back."

That reply snaps me to attention. "What does that mean?"

"Your mother went to see Gigi tonight," he says. "She was bitching about me, scared of me and she wanted to know why Gigi would bring me here. Once she left, Adam overheard Gigi call my father, and while she didn't talk to him, the message she left sounded pretty damning to Adam. Like they've been planning something together."

"Maybe Gigi and your father are trying to save the company together," I suggest, looking for a positive twist to this news, hoping this might be a bright spot. "She wants to save the company. She *is* his mother after all."

Eric's lips thin. "More like planning the end of us."

That statement punches me in the chest. Would Eric's own father plot to end him? No. Surely not. My hand comes down on his arm, my heart squeezing with what has to hurt him, but I never have a chance to speak. Savage jerks us into motion at the same moment that

Eric's phone rings. He snakes it from his pocket, glancing at the number and then me. "Adam."

He answers the call and listens a few minutes, talking back and forth with the other man, but with so few words, I can't read into what he's saying. "Your mother is at home in bed asleep," he says, when he disconnects, only to have his phone ring again. "Blake Walker," he says this time and as they settle into what feels like a non-eventful conversation, I sink back into my seat, confused by this new development with Gigi. Something isn't adding up. She told me his father had no idea she was asking Eric to come to Denver, or rather that *I* was asking Eric to come to Denver. Did she lie to me?

Eric disconnects his call and I jump on the chance to talk to him before he gets another. "Your father can't know about the attack."

"And you base this on what?"

"You're his son. You were being set-up."

"I'm his bastard son."

"Your head always goes there, doesn't it?"

"His sure does. That's the point."

"Okay. I don't like to think that's true, but assuming he does know, and I'm not convinced he does, make me understand why your father would come here and risk aligning himself with a murder plot."

"He wouldn't," Eric says. "But he's not here to help us, either. He's here to serve himself. He's here to protect himself."

Or Isaac, I think. "And hurt us?" I ask.

Eric takes my hand. "Yes. And to hurt us."

I'd argue with him but he knows his father better than I do. In six years, I've never even shared a cup of coffee with that man alone. "Coming here makes him look guilty. Maybe that's the idea. Maybe someone else baited him into coming here."

"You're reaching. Why are you protecting him?"

"He's your father."

Eric's lips thin and he cuts his stare before he looks back at me, those blue eyes hard, cold. "How have you been with this family this long and you don't see how evil they are?"

A chill rolls down my spine. "What does that mean? Whatever it is that you think is going on, just say it."

"My father's the kind of man who could easily sit next to us, sip a drink, and watch while we took bullets that he paid to put in us, but it doesn't stop there. He'd take one himself just to be sure he looks innocent. He's that devious. It's a mistake to assume he's here to do anything but end us, which is exactly why I'll end him first."

"End him? What does *that* mean?"

He cuts his stare, and I grab his arm, pulling him around to me. "*What* does that mean, Eric?"

CHAPTER TWELVE

Harper

Eric's eyes glint when they meet mine. "What does that mean?" I repeat. "End him? End your father?"

Those blue, blue eyes of his, such intelligent eyes, meet mine. "As we said in the Navy: All in, all the time. It's war. It's us or them. Me or him. I have to be willing to do whatever it takes to make sure it's me and us. I'm all in."

"You're avoiding a direct answer," I accuse. "You want to end him how?"

He shackles my arm and pulls me to him. "I want this fucking family out of my life and yours," he says, his voice low, rough. "And I want it to happen now."

"I do, too, but the right way."

"And what exactly is the right way, Harper? Do we let them kill you next time so they achieve whatever goal they set out to achieve when they were creating a bank account with your name on it?"

I shove against him and pull free, pointing at him. "Don't be an asshole."

"Just a bastard?"

"What is *wrong* with you?" I demand.

"It's called being born a Kingston."

The SUV jerks to a sharp halt that sends me backward. Eric catches me and pulls me to him and our faces end up close, his breath warm on my lips. "I got you, remember?"

I soften instantly, my hands settling on his chest. "And I have you. That's why I can't let you do something you'll regret."

"I'll do whatever it takes to end this," he says softly. "To protect you and if you hate me for it, hate me."

"I don't hate you." I lean back to look at him. "I'll never hate you, but please don't do something you'll regret."

The SUV starts moving again and then immediately halts. "Fucktard," Savage growls. "Red light means stop."

And just like that, Eric and I are laughing, and with that laughter, Eric's mood shifts, and I can sense that he finds a quiet spot in his head. He strokes my hair and casts me in a tender stare that spreads through me like warm sun on a winter's day, and with it is the promise that more warmth will follow.

There's a loud honk and Savage growls again. "Shoot that finger, you bastard. We both know that if I got out of this Escalade and Green Beret'd your ass, you'd be sucking your thumb."

Bastard.

I hate that word.

Eric laces his fingers with mine and winks. "Sometimes it takes a bastard to get the job done."

"Or get everyone's ass beat," Savage grumbles.

"Good point," I call out, giving Eric a "see" look.

Eric leans close. "But every bastard isn't me, sweetheart."

We share a look and in unison, we settle into our seats, our legs aligned and touching, our fingers laced together. There's laughter between us but that rough exchange of minutes before hasn't been forgotten. He was angry with his father but he was angry with me, too.

He'd asked me how I'd been in this family for this long and failed to see what his family is capable of. Does he think I did and looked the other way?

"I did know," I say, admitting the truth that I hadn't even realized was the truth until now. I shift to look at Eric, to own my mistakes. "I pretended I didn't know what this family was capable of because—I did. If I hadn't, maybe we wouldn't be here now. You wouldn't have gotten pulled into this."

His lips press together. "You didn't pull me into this. They did. They just used you as the tool to make it happen. Had you been out of the picture, they'd have found another way. I should have never left myself exposed. I won't again." He cuts his stare and I can feel him shutting me out and I don't know why.

"Together, remember?" I whisper.

That gets his attention. His eyes meet mine. "We are together." Three words that seem simple, spoken with this absolute quality that should please me but there's something unspoken there, too. Something not so simple, that I want to question, but Savage steals my chance.

"And we're here," he announces, pulling us to a stop in front of a building. "Alive and well despite the swampland of bad drivers."

Just that quickly, my conversation with Eric about his father and the Kingstons is over, at least for now. The doors to the SUV open on all sides, as valets attend to our service and the cold air has me hugging myself. The minute I'm out of the vehicle, and under a canopy, Eric's by my side, his arm wrapping around my shoulders, his big body warming mine as he introduces me to one of the doormen and then palms him a large tip. The man's eyes go wide and Eric and I laugh, exchanging a look that staves off all remnants of the chill I'd felt only seconds before. It warms me all over. Together. That's how we feel in this moment.

The doorman walks away, talking to Savage as Eric gives them his back, facing me, his fingers caressing my cheek, his touch both sandpaper and silk on my nerve endings. "Whatever you think is wrong right now, isn't." He kisses me soundly on the lips. "We're good and we're going to stay that way. That's a promise."

Before Eric can say another word, before I can reply to his promise, Savage is stepping between us. "Come to daddy, you two," he says, holding out his arms. "Tips delivered. Keys handed off. Where do I get a good whiskey?" He eyes Eric. "Your home bar, right?"

Eric and I both laugh at this man's outrageousness. "Yes," Eric assures him. "At my home bar." Eric drapes his arm around me as we enter the lobby of elegant white tiles and red cushioned chairs, to make our way to the elevators.

Once we're inside the car, Eric leans on the wall and pulls me to him, my back to his front, his hands on my hips.

The floors tick by and Savage hums, "We Wish You a Merry Christmas," when Halloween hasn't even arrived, and despite him looking like the hot, but mean guy, who'd never even consider singing a Christmas carol. But I tune out Savage and his song. I'm thinking about how done I believe Eric is with this family. So am I. I am, but I haven't suffered what he has. I don't believe they killed someone close to me as he does of them with his mother. I haven't lived his hell. I remember him denying this family was a part of him and then turning around and saying that he was done denying that he's a Kingston. I hope like hell he doesn't think that gives him a free pass to act like a Kingston considering the Kingstons just tried to kill me. Is that what he means by "end" his father?

Does he intend to kill him? Does he believe he's the one who ordered the hit on me and now he wants revenge?

I turn in Eric's arms, my hands settling on his chest, and I search his handsome, unreadable face, trying to understand where his head is right now. He arches a brow but offers me nothing. I don't find my answer, and I can't demand one with Savage in the car, so I repeat his words, from just a few minutes ago. *Whatever you think is wrong right now, isn't. We're good and we're going to stay that way. That's a promise.*

He promised.

And promises don't lie.

CHAPTER THIRTEEN

Harper

The elevator dings, the doors opening, and Savage exits first. When I would follow, Eric catches my arm and turns me to him, his hands coming down on my face. "Stop thinking yourself into a zoo with bars. I told you. We're okay."

"I know," I say. "You promised."

A flicker of understanding settles in his stare. "And you need to know that my promises mean something." He doesn't wait for me to reply. "They do." He catches my hand with his. "I promise they will end, but we will not." And with that statement, that only makes me more certain he's going to do something we'll both regret, he leads me into the hallway.

Savage is standing at the apartment door at the end of a long hallway. "I guess you can tell which one's mine," Eric says, casting me an amused look.

"He does have a way of getting his point across," I contend.

"Yes, he does," Eric agrees, and we quickly join the big goof of a man, that still makes it clear that he could kill you in two seconds flat.

"Heads up," Savage says, as we join him and Eric reaches for his key. "Several members of my team are inside waiting."

Eric eyes Savage over his shoulder. "You hacking my locks now, Savage? Because you know, if you hacked my locks I'll have to kill you."

"You'll have to kill me another day," Savage replies. "Grayson used his key."

That announcement is a nugget of welcome information. Grayson is not only here, he's close enough to Eric to have a key, and as a bonus, he's a voice of reason and morality. I know this from Eric's own admission. Grayson, who Eric also said grounded him and made him a better person, the person he likes to be. Grayson's presence, I welcome. Eric opens the door and pulls me in front of him, his hands scorching my waist, as he leans in close to whisper. "Welcome to my home."

In this moment, there is only me and him, and him and me. There is us and I can almost hear his wicked thoughts, and feel his hands on my body in places he's not touching. Savage clears his throat, and Eric shoves the door open. I enter a narrow hallway with black hardwood beneath my feet, looking up to find a giant black-rimmed oval clock on my left, and a magnificent painting of a jaguar on the right.

Eric steps to my side and catches my fingers with his, his eyes alight with mischief. "I saw that painting and just had to have it."

Because it reminds him of his enemy, his family, I think, even as he ironically says, "Now you meet my real family."

Grayson.

He means Grayson.

He kisses my knuckles, something warm and yet turbulent in his stare as Savage steps around us and heads down the hallway. "Has he been here before?" I ask.

"Never," Eric replies. "But he's Savage. He's—"

"Comfortable everywhere," I say and we both laugh, it's a light, welcome moment that carries us down the hallway with lighter steps.

"Come on," he says, guiding me forward and it's a short few feet before we pass an archway. I glance under it to find a long, black dining room table with a stunning painting of the jaguar on his arm behind it compelling me to stop and admire it, but I don't. That's for later, when we can talk about just how obsessed he is with the Kingston family. Because no matter what he claims, he is. There's no way he'd have a jaguar, the competition's icon, everywhere, if he wasn't.

For now, I allow Eric to urge me past that room, following the voices that sound ahead of us until we clear the walkway. I step into Eric's open-concept living room that connects to a kitchen by way of a granite island; it's a room of warm colors and masculine décor, with black leather furnishings, high-beamed ceilings and one wall that is nothing but windows. It fits him. I think maybe I do, too.

Savage and another man, one of the Walker team, I assume, are huddled up near a bar to the right of the kitchen. Two other men, both also casual in jeans and T-shirts, sit on the couch in deep conversation. Grayson is one of those men and he and the other man immediately stand and start walking toward us, joining us in a few short steps.

"What the hell are you doing here, Davis?" Eric demands, focusing on the "other" man.

"I'm your damn friend," Davis replies, his cursed rebuttal a contrast to his refined good looks and chiseled features. "I know you forget that, asshole," he snaps. "But I am."

"I don't have friends," Eric quips back and the energy between them tells me that this is just who they are together. They push and pull. They fight. "Right, Davis? Isn't that what you're always telling me?"

"Well then," Davis comments dryly, "I'm an enemy watching your fucking back." He glances at me. "Sorry. He just pissed me off and the word 'fuck' summed up how I felt too well to miss the opportunity to use it. I'm Davis. A close friend, attorney, and confidant to Grayson." He glances at Eric. "And you, asshole."

Grayson smirks, amusement in his eyes. "They really are friends," he assures me. "I promise you. And welcome back to New York, Harper." He takes my hand and covers it with his other hand, warmth in his touch that is all about that welcome he just expressed. "I'm glad you came back with Eric."

"Me, too," I say, and when he releases me, I look at Eric and repeat the words, "Me, too," and with good reason. These men are his friends. I want them to know that I'm one hundred percent on Eric's side. I'm not a Kingston. I'm not a damn princess.

Eric touches my cheek, approval in his eyes before he glances at Grayson. "My father is on his way here."

"I heard," he confirms, "and I think we should talk about where that leads you."

"Me, too," I chime in again, squeezing Eric's hand, but he doesn't look at me.

"We'll talk, all right," he replies, his tone steel as he eyes Savage. "What do we know about my father's trip?"

The group of us spread out and form a circle to the side of the couches, and Savage and the man he's been talking with—a tall, dark-haired man with long hair tied at his nape, join us. "This is Blake," Savage says indicating the other man. "One of the Walker brothers. That means one of my bosses. He's also a world-class hacker. I'm not. I'm still just brute force me."

"The one who hacked me to freedom," I assume.

Blake's attention shifts to me. "If you mean I got rid of the bank account that was created in your name, yes."

"Thank you. Thank you so much," I say."

Blake gives me a nod and then focuses on Eric, getting right to business "We know your father had an argument with your brother at the warehouse before he booked his trip. When he left the warehouse, he called no one but his assistant, who booked his trip. He's in the air now and hasn't communicated with anyone in transit. At least not on a known device that we're tracking. He could have burner phones or unregistered electronics."

Eric eyes Savage and Blake. "Let's step outside." He doesn't wait for their agreement. He starts walking, decisively, determined, as if he has a plan and he's setting it in motion and that's enough for me to decide this could be trouble. I can't let this meeting happen before I talk to him. I don't know Walker Security. I don't know what they'll do or agree to. I don't know where Eric's endgame lands him, or where his head is right now, but I know that I don't want to find out the wrong way and too late to stop a disaster.

I dash forward and I place myself in front of Eric, planting my hands on his chest. "We need to talk before you say another word to anyone."

His eyes narrow and glint hard. "Why?"

Because he blames his father for killing his mother and now for my attack. Because I think he's secretly wanted to end that man for his entire life. He hates his father far too much for me to let him make any decisions tonight, when all those old wounds have been cut open to bleed anew.

But I can't say those things and have him listen.

I need a reason to get him into another room alone and I make a fast decision that now is the time to put it all on the line. Now is the time for me to stop holding back and I act on that decision before I can back out. "Because I need to tell you something. I need to talk to you."

He studies me for several long beats, his expression unreadable, before he takes my hands and starts walking across the room without speaking a word to any of the men in the room. His strides are long, calculated and rapid enough to have my short legs struggling to keep up. Once we're on the stairs, he places me in front of him and I hurry forward, hyperaware of this man at my back. Hyperaware of the box I just shoved myself inside, and how easily a box can be cut open and destroyed.

We travel up a winding set of stairs and when we reach the top level it's a few steps until we enter a pair of open double doors. I have about ten seconds to take in a massive black-framed bed on a pedestal before the doors shut behind me. Another ten seconds before Eric has placed me against the door and steps in front of me, his powerful thighs caging mine, his palms flattening on the door on either side of me. "I'm listening."

He's listening.

And now I need to talk.

Now I need to tell him what I brought him up here to tell him.

Officially, my time is up.

CHAPTER FOURTEEN

Harper

I stand there against the wall with Eric's big body framing mine and those intelligent, blue eyes fixed on my face, waiting for me to tell him what I declared he must know urgently. He's beautiful. He's gifted. He's damaged in ways that I wasn't equipped to understand six years ago. In ways that I can never fully understand, but I know drive his actions now, with the way this family has targeted us both. Because he's also a fighter, a warrior, a Navy SEAL who has fought to the death. While I find this part of him brutally sexy, it's also terrifying right here, right now, with his talk of ending his father.

"Talk to me, Harper," he urges, his voice low, almost gentle, but tension radiates off of him, almost as if it pings off the walls and slams right back into him.

I press my hand to the solid wall of his chest and his heart thunders under my touch. Because of my touch? Because of what he's about to do to end his father? "Whatever you were about to tell Walker Security to do down there, please don't."

He offers no denial. His hand comes down on mine, his piercing eyes capturing mine. "Why would you protect my father?"

There's an accusation in that question that pisses me off. "Are you really serious right now? I'm not protecting your father," I say. "I'm protecting *you*."

"Me? How are you protecting me, Harper?"

"There are some things you can't come back from."

"What do you think I'm about to do?"

"Tell me. What are you about to do?"

"Whatever it fucking takes to get that man out of our lives once and for all."

"Kill him?" I challenge. "Would you *kill* him?"

"Kill or be killed, sweetheart. I'll do whatever it takes." He is cold, hard, decisive. He's made up his mind. He has a plan and it's a plan I have to change.

"No," I hiss, bunching his shirt in my free hand. "No, you will not."

"You don't want him to die."

Again with his damn accusations. "I don't want *you* to die. Do you really think you could live with killing your father?"

"Live with it? I'd sleep like a baby if that man was gone. What don't I know *again,* Harper? What did you bring me up here to confess?"

"Confess?" My anger ignites all over again. "I have nothing to confess. You already know what I have to say. There is no secret. There is no *again.* I *hate* that you just said that to me. But I guess there is an *again* because I wanted you alone so that I could say something to you that I said on the phone. Something I thought you needed to hear again, live and in person."

His jaw spasms and he looks right, seeming to struggle before he fixes me in a turbulent stare. "You know you teased me with a secret to get me up here."

"I didn't."

"You did. Don't throw out taunts about secrets with me, Harper. Not now. Not after what we went through tonight."

"Me? Look who's talking. Don't you accuse me of keeping secrets and taunting you. I never taunted you and I never kept a secret that I wanted to keep. I promised you on the plane that I have no more secrets."

"You know you used the promise of another one to get me up here."

I ball his shirt as tight as possible in my hand and step into him. "I said I had something you needed to hear."

"I'm still listening," he says. "I'm still waiting."

And here it is. That moment of truth I committed to when I brought him up here. "I have needed you since the moment we met and no amount of time or space would ever erase the impact you've had on me. You *affect me.* You scare me. You own me in ways I don't want to be owned, and yet I do with you. If you do this, if you go at your father in the way I know you want to tonight, I'll lose you again. And I don't want to lose you again. I just found you."

He doesn't immediately reply.

He stares down at me, his eyes hooded, his expression inscrutable, seconds ticking by in which I start to fear I've said too much. I start to fear I've asked for too much. Time and his silence close in on me with such heaviness that I can't breathe, but then he's molding me to him, his fingers splayed on my lower back. "I've been obsessed with you since the moment I saw you across that pool, Harper. You affect me, too. You belong with me and I'm not losing you again." His mouth closes down on mine, brutal and punishing, hot and seductive, long strokes of his tongue caressing mine until I can barely breathe. When he finally relents, his hand moves roughly over my breast, and his lips linger above mine, his breath hot, and his voice a near growl. "You're mine now, Harper. I own you. No one gets to take you from me. You understand? No one."

His emotions pound on me, punishing me like his kiss, the way he wants to punish them. "Eric—"

85

"They tried to kill you tonight, Harper. I believe that. You aren't the one who ends up dead."

"If you kill your father or your brother, you could go to jail. Then I lose you again."

"I'm way better than a common criminal, sweetheart. I won't go to jail."

Those words punish me yet again. He's brutal. He's a killer. And I love him. I do. I love him. "What if Walker screws up?"

"Walker won't know. I handle my own dirty work. I'm going to handle this and then I'm going to come back up here and fuck you in my bed just like I promised. And the word 'again' applies because I'm going to fuck you, lick you, and kiss you, again and again." His fingers tangle in my hair, rough and erotic. "You're never going to want to leave my bed. That's a promise." And then he's kissing me again, sealing that promise with a deep, demanding stroke of his tongue before he orders, "Stay here," and he moves me, setting me away from the door.

I'm instantly cold, ice in my veins freezing every inch of me. He's already reaching for the door, and I can't let him leave. I dart forward and place myself between the door and him again. "You will not kill anyone. That's an order."

He tangles his fingers in my hair again. "You will not say those words again. You will not speak of murder. You will not speak of any of this. Understand?"

"No. No, I don't understand. You will not—"

His turns me toward the door, pressing my hands on the hard surface, framing my body with his. "You will not repeat those words. Ever."

"I'm not agreeing to that," I pant out.

He shoves my hands over my head. "Damn it, Harper. You will listen to me." He buries his face in my neck. "You will listen or I swear I'll make you listen."

There's an erotic promise in those words that shouldn't turn me on, not in the context he speaks them, but they do. They so do. "Make me then," I challenge, welcoming whatever that means, my sex aching, wet. My nipples puckered and throbbing. I want whatever he's offering. I want him here with me.

His hands slide over my waist, cupping my breasts, pinching my nipples through my shirt and bra. "I should," he whispers. "I really fucking should, but I'm not going to. Not like this. Not when I'm like this. Fuck." He pushes away from me, leaving my sex aching and wet, my body screaming for some unknown pleasure it's been denied.

I rotate to find him standing with his back to me, his hand at the back of his neck. "Fuck," he curses again, turning to me. "What the hell are you doing to me, woman?"

His eyes are dark, stormy, his body a hard line of edgy need. I want to understand that need. I want to understand this man. I want to satisfy the burn in him for revenge, and I know only one way to do that. To satisfy another need in him, to drive him over the edge, and then bring him down, and then maybe, just maybe, he'll let go of his anger to see a solution that doesn't include murder. Maybe I'll save him and us. That means now, before he puts something in motion I can't stop.

"You can't leave this room yet," I say. "I won't let you."

"You can't stop me, Harper."

He's wrong. I can and I will.

CHAPTER FIFTEEN

Harper

I'm still against the door of Eric's bedroom, my body all that's stopping him from leaving this room and acting on his promise to end his father. My declaration that he's not leaving the room between us. His declaration that I can't stop him, right there with it. And he's right, of course. I can't stop him. Not if he really wants to leave. The man is six-foot-two or three at least, and a wall of solid, hot, hard muscle. He has that control. He is, in fact, one hundred percent in control of the physical equation. He's in control of what happens next if he wants to be, and that's a problem because I know, *I know*, that if I let him leave this room right now, I won't be able to stop him from acting against his father. I don't know the right move to make to deal with the hell we're in, but I know with certainty that making any move right now, in his current state of mind, is not a decision made of the genius he was born with.

It's emotional.

It's passionate.

It's about pain, revenge, and anger.

It's about the attempt on my life that I can't think about right now. If I crumble, he'll act out. He'll lash out. He'll protect me at all costs, and the costs could be too high. He'd do all this for me and that affects me on so many levels, in so many ways. No one but this man would do anything for me, and the fact that he would is a realization that warms me, but also comes with responsibility for how I affect his actions.

I'm suddenly ravenous to tear away Eric's physical control, to find the man beneath all those emotions and all that powerful anger. Desperate to save him the way he saved me because I know no matter what his claim, he'd regret the actions he's planned against his father. He might be a genius, but he's still just a man, and a man I want the chance to know; all of him, all of the broken, damaged pieces beneath his perfect surface. I'm not letting him out of this room until I know what is really in his head or until he at least promises me to wait to make any decision that doesn't involve us naked in his bed.

I go to him and I don't give him time to react, my hands catching at his waist. "You say I belong with you."

"You *do* belong with me." His tone is absolute, his voice and eyes pure steel.

"That means *you* belong with *me*."

"Yes, Harper. It does." He says those words without hesitation, his voice low, a raspy hint to it, that says he's affected and yet, he doesn't touch me.

A charge hums from him, like a ball of anger spinning in the air, faster and faster until it combusts. Like years of anger and pain that have collided into this moment, this piece of time and I understand. He walked away. He made his own future and yet still they came for him— God, *I* came for him. They've pushed his limits and he needs to find them again.

I need to find them for him.

I drop to my knees and caress the thick ridge of his erection. He's hard, thick, pulsing beneath the stretch of his zipper. He wants me. He needs me like he did on the plane and I believe now that he just needs a release. He needs to fuck or be fucked. No. He needs to take and I need to give.

"What are you doing, Harper?"

"Giving you a reason to stay in this room with me." I reach for his belt and tug it free.

He catches my shoulders, finally touching me. God, I didn't know how much I needed him to touch me, to prove to me that he's here, he's still in this room with me. "People are waiting on us," he warns, staring down at me, his eyes hooded, heavy.

"They'll wait," I say, unzipping his pants, aware that he hasn't pushed me away or pulled me to my feet. "We both know what you need right now."

"What do I need, Harper?"

"To take a pause. To breathe again. To get out of your own head."

I reach beneath his pants, my hand finding the hard, warm flesh of his erection as I ease him from his clothes. And the fact that he doesn't stop me empowers me. As does the carnal look on his face as he watches me. I like that look, oh yes, I do. Just as I like how hot and hard he is in my palm, and the way liquid pools at the tip of his cock. Boldly, I catch his stare before I give him a long, sensual lick.

He shuts his eyes, his lashes low, his body tight, but he's not touching me again. He's trying to maintain control. He's trying to keep it as his own and that I don't like. I lick his cock again, swirling my tongue all over him, around him, up and down, and when I suck hard and deep, a soft breath escapes his lips. A breath he tries to control but can't. Encouraged now, I take just the tip of him in my mouth and suckle hard, but I don't take more, I make him want and need, but he can't have it, not yet. Not until I get what I want. Not until he's one hundred percent in the moment.

I lick and swirl, thrusting my tongue down the underside of him, and finally, his fingers tangle in my hair. Finally, he's all in. "Holy fuck, woman," he growls. "You know you're killing me. Take all of me."

Take all of him.

Oh yes. I will.

Heat pools low in my belly and my nipples pucker and ache. I want and need just as he does. I want his control. I want his revenge. I want his anger. I want it all right here, right in this moment. I suck him deep and hard. I suck him and clutch him and move up and down him.

"Yes," he murmurs. "Deeper, Harper."

Harper.

I have no idea why him using my name right now has me on the verge of orgasm, but it does. I've never been this wet and hot from giving a blow job. My lips tighten around his shaft, and I slide all the way to my fingers where they grip him. He thrusts into my mouth and a salty-sweet taste touches my tongue. He's close. He's right there where I want him and I pump my hand against his next thrust, and repeat. Again. Again. And then again until the muscles of his thigh that are now under my palm lock up, even as his fingers tighten in my hair.

"Deeper," he demands again. "More."

More.

He wants more and more works for me. My breasts are heavy, my sex dripping, I'm so very wet.

I pump my hand again and stroke my tongue low and high. He pumps into my mouth and then he's shuddering, the salty taste of his release exploding in my mouth, a low groan sliding from his lips. And incredulously, I come. I come with him and I didn't know that was possible, but I do. And when it's over, my forehead is on his stomach, my body weak. The next thing I know, I'm on my feet, Eric's hands on my shoulders, his eyes locked with mine.

"If you're trying to make me fall in love with you, Harper it's working, but that doesn't save my father or that family. You can't save them. Not this time." He sets me away from him and this time when he heads for the door, I can't stop him.

I whirl around just in time to watch him exit the room.

LISA RENEE JONES

CHAPTER SIXTEEN

Harper

I don't stand in the bedroom and hope for the best. I'm out the room and on Eric's heels in the blink of an eye. I don't call after him, though. Not yet. Not with a houseful of people and I doubt I'll stop him at this point anyway. He believes he's protecting me. Now, I need to protect him. He clears the stairs before I do and by the time I'm around the corner, Eric is following the Walker team toward the front door.

"Eric!" I call out.

Much to my relief, he stops walking but he doesn't turn, tension tracking his shoulders down to his fingers where they curl into his palms at his sides. I'm not discouraged. I hurry forward and I step in front of him, planting my hand over his chest, holding him right here with me. "Where are you going?"

"You knew I needed to talk to the Walker team."

"Talk? Just talk? Or make plans that you can't come back from?" I don't give him time to reply. "Promise me you won't take any permanent actions until we can talk."

"We'll talk," he replies, his expression inscrutable.

"That's a not a promise. I need a promise, Eric."

There's a flex in his jaw before he's suddenly dragging me to him, his hands firmly on my waist. "Bastards don't make promises they actually keep."

"Then don't be a bastard, because we both know that's your choice. You told me your promises matter."

"I swear to you, princess, if you—"

"Don't finish that sentence and turn into a bastard by choice. If you do, we're going to end up fighting right here in the middle of all these men. I'm trying to protect you."

"What the hell do you think I'm trying to do?"

"Protect me. I know that." I meet his stare. "*I know.* Make the promise."

He cups my head and kisses me. "I promise," he says. "For you. *Only* for you." His voice is low, gravelly. Rough. "I won't be long."

I don't get to ask him where he's going or what he's doing. He sets me aside and heads for the door, but I let him leave this time. He made me a promise and I trust him to keep it. The door opens and shuts behind me and that's when I find myself in the spotlight. Grayson and Davis are standing in the living room, watching me.

Davis arches a brow. "That was something to observe."

"What are you talking about?" I ask, confused.

"You," Davis replies. "Eric. I'm not used to seeing him invested in a woman."

"He's known me a long time," I say, closing the space between the other two men and me. "For all kinds of reasons. I'm his stepsister. I'm his—"

"Woman," Grayson amends, his voice low, but no less absolute. "You're *the woman*. I saw it in his eyes when he looked at you. And I saw him in your eyes when you looked at him. I knew the day you came to the office." He motions toward a bar on the wall next to the patio door. "Drink?" He doesn't give me time to reply to his stunning revelation. He walks to the bar and Davis joins him, but my gaze locks on that door next to them, on the patio entrance.

Eric had planned to talk to the Walker men out there before we went upstairs. Instead, he left with them. He made sure I couldn't interrupt this time. He promised me he wouldn't do anything permanent before we talked, and yet, he didn't go to the patio. He left the apartment.

He promised me.

He wouldn't break his promise.

Grayson hands me a glass. "Drink. It'll help calm your nerves. You've been through a lot tonight."

"I'm not worried about me."

"Let Eric do what he needs to do to make sure this ends sooner rather than later."

"He wants to end it by ending his father."

"He's wanted to end his father for a very long time. He didn't do it. He has reasons not to do it."

"Because of his mother, I know, but he believes they tried to kill me tonight, Grayson. He wants his father dead."

"He promised you he'd talk to you before he did anything permanent. I heard him."

"That's all you're going to say? He wants to *kill* him."

He eyes Davis and Davis nods. "I actually need to deal with a client at the office. I may or may not be back." He glances at me. "He's intense. It's contagious. Drink the drink." He turns and walks away.

I frown and eye Grayson. "Did he just tell me I'm wound too tightly?"

He chuckles. "I do believe he did." He motions to my drink.

"I know. Drink it. It'll help. I'm following the theme going on here, but I'm not a good drinker. I need a clear mind right now for Eric."

"Eric isn't going anywhere without you. You were attacked. You could have ended up dead. He is not leaving your side. His father is safe for the night. He's not on his way to kill his father. The man is still in an airplane."

"Do you believe he'd do it?"

"Not tonight, and I know him. By morning, he'll decide death is too good for him."

"How can you be so sure?"

"Because I met him when he was still bleeding out over his mother's death, and even then, he didn't go after the family. His mother's wishes meant too much to him."

"They went after him through me. They went after *me*. He knows this. He's not going to let that go. I feel it. I see it in his eyes."

"He promised you that he wouldn't act. You proved you have the power to affect his decisions."

I down my drink. "You just put the world on my shoulders."

"No," he says. "The world is on his shoulders and has been for a very long time. You can ease that pressure. You can make him let go of the past once and for all."

"I'm part of his past. I'm part of *them* and he hates that."

"He's a part of them, too, but both of you can choose to walk away."

"*They won't let us,* Grayson. I believe in my heart that they tricked me into setting him up for my own murder." Saying that out loud to someone other than Eric twists me in knots. "I need another drink. No. I need Eric here. Now." I reach for my phone and remember that I don't have it. "I have no phone. I have no purse. I have no clothes."

"My wife, Mia, is bringing you some necessities, including a new phone."

"Because Eric's like a brother to you and you're protecting me to protect him."

His eyes warm with that statement. "Eric is my brother."

Brother.

That word radiates through me and I walk to the bar myself, refill my glass and down it again. "I believe he's hit a limit," I say when Grayson offers me his glass to fill. "If you really love him like a brother—"

"I do," he says, taking the whiskey in my hand from me.

"Help me stop him."

"What are you suggesting?"

"I don't know, Grayson. I just know if he does this, he'll lose sleep. He'll feel pain over it. Even if he doesn't get caught—"

"I wouldn't get caught."

At the sound of Eric's voice, I whirl around to find him standing a few feet away and relief washes over me. He's back. He's already back.

"And I told you, Harper. I would sleep just fine, but I don't plan to kill him or anyone. That would be too gentle a punishment." His cellphone rings and he pulls it from his pocket to glance at the number. His expression is stone, his entire body more stone than man, as he allows seconds to count down before he answers the call.

He takes the call, gives a clipped greeting, listens several seconds and then says, "When?" Another few beats pass and he adds, "I'll be there." He disconnects the line and cuts his stare, seeming to think, perhaps calming his mind a moment, before he says, "I'll be back," and turns and heads for the door.

Warning bells go off in my head and I run for him, planting myself between him and the door, watching him slip into a jacket. "Who was that, Eric?"

"My father." He opens a drawer to the foyer table, pulls out a gun, checks it, and sticks it in his pants.

"You need a gun?"

He faces me, his stance wide. "Would you rather me go without one after what happened at the warehouse?"

"You're not going to meet him. Not tonight. Sleep this off. Think about what comes next."

"I don't need to think."

"You aren't going to meet him."

"Yes," he says. "I am." And once again, he sets me aside, opens the door, and leaves.

I try to follow, but Savage steps in my path. "Sorry, honeybunch. I can't let you leave."

"Move, Savage, or I will hurt you."

He arches a brow. "You do appreciate the ridiculousness of that statement, I'm sure." He steps back just enough to indicate another man with sandy brown hair and lots of muscles, standing beside him. "I even have back up. This is Smith. He's going to be your regular doorman."

Smith gives me a nod, confirming that I'm outnumbered. I grimace and turn back to the apartment. Grayson appears in the foyer and I look at him. "He went to meet his father. He won't kill him, right?"

Grayson's eyes darken. "That's not his plan."

"That's not a no."

"It's the only answer I have for you."

CHAPTER SEVENTEEN

Eric

The past...

Jennie pulls her giant truck to the edge of the trailer park and stops. "I have to let you off here." She looks at her watch. "Hurry. You have to go. I'm *so* late to work, it's insane. If I get fired, my mom will be pissed and we won't be going out this weekend."

"We aren't going out this weekend," I say. "You know that. I'm staying with my mother."

"You're only sixteen. You still have to live."

"What part of she's dying do you not understand?"

"I can't date a guy that can never date."

I cut her a look. "Then don't date me." I open the car door.

"Eric, damn it."

I don't reply. I get out of the truck. "Thanks for the ride." I slam the door and slide my backpack onto my shoulder. I have homework that will take me all of about thirty minutes. I can do it in the morning before class, but my mother likes to see me open books. I'll open them for her.

I start down the road that leads to our trailer, and just that easily, I'm already done with Jennie. I don't need anyone in my life right now but my mother anyway. I don't know why I tried. My mother is what matters. My mother who can't die. We have to find another treatment. There has to be a way to pay for it. I'll volunteer as a guinea pig. I'll let them study my brain. I know my mom doesn't want that, but she'll have to understand.

I turn the corner to our street and the sight of ambulances and fire trucks slams into me. My heart explodes in my chest. My stomach knots. Numbers begin to pound at my mind. "Mom. Mom!" I charge forward, blood pumping through my veins and in my ears. "Mom!" I run and run and I don't stop until I'm right on the edge of the yard and only then because a monster of a police officer catches my arms.

"Son," he orders. "You need to stay right here."

"I live here. I live here! This is my home. You can't stop me from going into my own home."

"Are you Eric Mitchell?"

"Yes." Tears start streaming down my cheeks. "I need to see my mother. She's sick. She's got cancer. She needs me. I'm her son!"

The officer hits a button on his arm and says, "Get that social worker here now."

"Social worker?! I don't need a social worker. I know she has cancer. What's wrong? Is it a reaction to the chemo? *What's wrong*?!"

"Son," he says, his voice vibrating with an undercurrent that touches his eyes. With something he doesn't want to say. "Son, your mother—"

"She's dead. She's dead, isn't she?"

He doesn't have to reply. I see it in his face and the numbers attack my mind, diving at it like sharp blades.

My knees go weak and I fall down, grabbing my head and in a tunnel of pain, I hear, "Get me an EMT tech! Now!"

I black out.

No. I don't black out. There are numbers.

11111
77777
88888
99999
11111

They won't stop. God, make them stop. I sit up, ramrod stiff and find myself in the back of an ambulance. "Easy, son," a male voice says, and I bring him into focus, sitting next to me. "I gave you something to calm you down."

"I don't want to calm down." I sit up. "I want to see my mother."

A woman with long brown hair in her mid-fifties appears at the end of the truck. "Eric, she's gone. I'm sorry."

I swallow hard, and try to find the numbers again, the ones I control but I can't find them. "How? How did she die?"

"She was in a lot of pain. She took her own life. "

"No. No, she was fighting. *She was fighting!*"

"She was tired. She wanted more for you, too. She left a letter. I called your father and—"

"I don't have a father. I don't fucking have a father!" I try to get up, but the EMT holds me down, my head spinning with the damn drug he gave me.

"I want to see the letter," I whisper.

"At my office," the woman says.

"Who are you?"

"Evelyn Minor. Your social worker." She holds out a hand. "Come with me."

Two hours later, I sit in her dingy office with a scuffed desk and yellow chair, the letter in hand, but no numbers in my head. That drug the EMT gave me makes me dizzy again as I start reading:

My dearest Eric—

I had to do this. I had to do it because I love you with all my heart and soul. I did this for you. It was time for you to get on with your life. It was time for your father to claim you. Make him. Accept him. He can help you make the most of your gifts. He can get you the help you need to control it. Don't fight him. Don't lash out at him. Do this for me. Do this so that I know I left you behind better than I brought you into this world. Please, son. I beg of you. I need you to do this. For me. Do this for me.

Before I can read on, the door to the office opens and in walks a man in a blue suit, his brown hair slicked back. I know him. I don't want to know him. Jeff Kingston, the man my mother claims is my father, ignores the social worker and steps in front of me, towering above me. "Looks like your mother got her way," he bites out. "You're with me now. Let's go."

"Excuse me," the social worker says. "But there's paperwork and—"

"Fuck your paperwork. Sue me if you want to. He's coming with me." He motions to me. "Get up. Come with me. Now."

No words of sorrow or sympathy.

Just a command.

And I have no choice but to follow it. It's what my mother wanted and she's gone. She's dead. She killed herself and any version of me that I knew.

104

THE PRINCESS

Present day...

I'm still standing in the foyer of Eric's apartment with Savage and Smith just outside the door, and Grayson standing in front of me, dismissing my worries about Eric and his father. "I thought you were the level-headed brother Eric values," I say to Grayson. "He doesn't plan on killing his father, but *hey, if it happens, it happens*, is not level-headed."

"I didn't say if it happens, it happens," Grayson replies, his tone cool but his voice is still low.

"You aren't worried at all. If you are, you hide it well."

"I know Eric well enough to know that he'll do the right thing."

"The right thing? How do you define the right thing when staring into the face of a man who just tried to frame you for the murder of your girlfriend? Call him. Call him now so he'll answer and let me talk to him."

"I'm not going to call him," he says. "He needs to focus. Someone tried to kill you. He could be the next target."

"All the more reason for him to be here. Call him."

There's a knock on the door and then it opens. "Hi," a female voice says, and a pretty brunette walks in with bags in her hand, a pretty green chiffon dress floating around her legs, her eyes finding mine. "Shopping trip successful. My favorite personal shopper worked miracles and got the stores to open for me. Did you know that Apple has a twenty-four hour store in Manhattan? Amazing. Oh." She laughs. "I guess I should introduce myself. I'm Mia. Grayson's wife. Nice to meet you, Harper." She sets the bags down. "I brought you some necessities."

The door shuts behind her and I give her my full attention, but introductions are the last thing on my mind. "Tell him to call Eric. Tell him."

"What?" Mia looks at Grayson. "What's going on?"

"Someone tried to kill me and frame Eric," I say, not sure what she knows. "Eric wants to 'end' his father, and now his father is here, in the city. He went to meet him. I couldn't stop him."

Mia looks between me and Grayson. "End him how?"

"Kill him," I say. "I think he wants him dead."

"He won't kill him," Grayson bites out. "He's got this under control."

"He was quaking, literally, after he found out about his father. That is not under control."

"Quaking?" Grayson demands.

"Yes. His entire body was trembling, and I know it was one of those attacks he used to have trying to come back."

He narrows his eyes on me. "You know about the attacks?"

"Yes. I know. He isn't good right now."

"My God, Grayson," Mia says. "If he's that bad and she's as bonded to him as you told me she is, then let her call him. Get him back. Make sure he's okay."

Grayson stares at Mia, seconds ticking by before he pulls his phone from his pocket and punches a number before handing it to me. "It's ringing."

I eagerly take the phone and listen as the ringing continues, and then goes to voicemail. "Eric," I breathe out. "Please come back. Don't meet with him tonight. Talk to me. Be with me. Take a breath and just think. Please. I need you and I don't want to lose you." I hang up and redial, but it goes to voicemail again. This time when the line beeps, I say, "Please come back to me, now, before you meet with him."

I disconnect and hand the phone back to Grayson before I walk into the living room, barely seeing the room, my destination the floor-to-ceiling windows. I stop at the glass and stare out at the inky night, not a star in the sky. There is just the darkness eating away at Eric, and holding us captive.

CHAPTER EIGHTEEN

Harper

Fifteen minutes after Eric leaves me in his apartment with Grayson and Mia, I'm fretting and then fretting some more over where he is and what he's doing. I'm also still standing at the window of Eric's apartment, watching the fog expand and consume all remnants of the city lights. The way this family consumes both Eric and my mother. "He's one of the strongest people I've ever known," Grayson says, stepping to my side.

"But he's human," I argue, turning to face him.

"Barely," he replies softly. "More so with you in the picture."

"I thought you were more than his moral compass. I thought you were his best friend?"

"Part of being his friend is seeing him clearly."

"And yet you just said he's barely human. He's always human."

"He doesn't think like you and me. He lives with numbers first, and people second."

"Those numbers are his wall, his shield he hides behind and inside. And while it's hard to explain why, I know him. I understand him, and in his mind, those numbers tell one story over and over. The Kingston family killed his mother, the only person he's ever loved, besides you. Distance and your friendship allowed him to bank that, to compartmentalize his pain, but they pulled him back into their world. They brought it to the surface." My fist balls on my chest. "And I helped them." I turn back to the glass and press my hands to the bar there. "I came here to get him. I helped set this in motion."

"You didn't know you were being used."

I can't even look at him for the guilt spiraling inside me, a sharp blade that won't stop cutting me. "I should have known. I knew the family couldn't be trusted."

"My understanding is that's exactly why you went to Eric. Because you knew they couldn't be trusted and you felt he could help. And he is helping. He's the reason you're alive right now."

"I have coffee," Mia exclaims, joining us, two mugs in her hands, one that she hands me and another that she hands Grayson.

"Thank you," I say, accepting the mug. "I think I'm going to lose my mind if I don't calm my nerves. I'm really worried." I eye Grayson. "He told me he hasn't had an attack in years."

"Not since college," Grayson confirms.

"But he did today. Driven by the emotional trigger of his father. That was obvious."

He eyes Mia and seems to share a silent conversation with her before he refocuses on me. "The last time I saw him like that, he left Harvard the next day. He knew Isaac was pushing his buttons. He put distance between the two of them. He removed the triggers."

This comment doesn't take me to a good place. "And yet he knew his father was a trigger, and he just went right to him."

"He's not a college kid anymore," Grayson reminds me. "He's a man who walks into problems, rather than away from them. I know this. I see it every day."

"Is that good or bad?" Mia queries, crossing her arms in front of her. "Because if he really cares about Harper, and they, the Kingstons, I assume, tried to hurt her, the numbers in his head may calculate the odds of them succeeding next time as too risky. He might take the action, but the wrong action. We both know how much he hates that family." She looks at Grayson. "A man held me at gunpoint and you tried to get him to shoot you instead of me. Think about Eric doing the same."

I don't know what she's talking about, or who held a gun to her head and I don't ask. I can think of only one thing. She just said that Grayson tried to take a bullet for her. "Eric's trying to take the bullet for me, too, in some way, shape or form." I take a sip of my coffee, just to do something, anything. "I need the phone to try to call him again."

Grayson breathes out, scrubbing his jaw and dialing the number before handing it to me. It rings and rings, and I walk to a coffee table of black stone—a part of the black theme to the room that is as dark as I believe Eric's past is—and set my mug down. Voicemail picks up and I leave a message he may never hear. "I need you to come back here alive right now. I need you, period. I do. Come back so I can tell you that in person." I disconnect and dial again, and again, I get voicemail.

Grayson and Mia are looking at me when I hang up and Mia walks toward me. "Let's busy ourselves unpacking what I brought you so you won't worry. Or so you'll fill up some of the space in your mind where the worry wants to live."

A space the size of the city.

"I have such a bad feeling about this night," I whisper.

"He *will* be back and safe," Mia promises me.

I need her to be right.

No.

I just need Eric. Here. Now.

Eric

In the short time it takes for me to get an uneventful update from Adam, and exit my apartment building alone, my phone rings with a call from Grayson. "Sorry, brother," I murmur. "Not now." I hit decline. If anything important is happening, the Walker team will contact me

I place the phone on mute and cut right, walking toward my father's hotel, bypassing the use of a hired car with a driver that might remember my travels. I push through the fog-laden, cold night for another three blocks and once I'm at the hotel, I dial my father.

"Back of the building in the alleyway."

He snorts. "I'm not meeting you in the back of the hotel."

Just the sound of his voice cuts me all the way to my black soul he helped create. "You afraid of the dark? Good thing I'm not or Harper would be in a dark warehouse dead right now."

"I heard what happened, son. Why do you think I'm here?"

"You mean you ordered someone to kill her." It's not a question.

"You're confused, son," he says, using a familiar snide tone, "which is why we need to talk. Here. Now. In my room."

"Not a chance in hell, even your version of hell, where you're the devil that always gets his way. You have five minutes and then I'm gone. Back service door." I disconnect the line and a notification pops up with a voicemail from Grayson. I ignore it and head down the alleyway toward the back of the building. If my father won't come to me, I'll go to him, but on my terms, in my way. I walk to the back of the building, finding the alleyway dark, with a dim overhead light spiraling down on a dumpster. I take a position in a dark corner by the door I've named, where I'll wait to discover how desperate my father is to talk to me.

Three minutes pass and I become aware of someone else in the alleyway and he isn't my father. He is, however, dressed in all back. He steps behind the trashcan and disappears. Waiting on someone, and of course that someone is me.

CHAPTER NINETEEN

Eric

The past...

I leave the social worker's office on the heels of my father, who never looks back at me. When we get to his fancy car, he flicks me a look. "Backseat."

His message is clear: I don't belong in the front with him. I want to punch him. I want to hurt him like I know he hurt my mom. God, I want to kill him. He must see it in my face, too, because he charges up to me, grabs my shirt and shoves me against the car. "You got a problem with me, boy?"

"You're an asshole."

"Yes. I am. I'll teach you how to do it just like me and then maybe you'll belong with us. Right now, you don't. You forget that—you won't like the results. *Backseat.*" He releases me and walks to the front of the car.

I consider leaving, but my mother's letter is still in my hand. She wanted this for me. She wanted him for me. I get in the car and when I settle into the backseat, my "father" says, "People die. You're going to have to deal with it."

A swell of anger and pain fills my chest and I cut my gaze to the window. He starts the engine and I fight the burn of tears in my eyes. I won't cry in front of him. Once we're moving, I open the letter again and the first thing I read is: *You will not fight your father. You will not go after him or anyone in the family. You're smart enough to do it. You're smart enough to hurt them, but DON'T DO IT. That is my final wish. That is my plea to you. Don't do it. Because family doesn't hurt family and they're your blood, they're your family now, until we meet again one day in a better place.*

Present Day...

My father did exactly what I expected.

He hired someone to shut me up, if not kill me.

If my mother was alive, if she'd written that letter she wrote me so many years ago, knowing what I now know, she'd show the side of her that was a fighter. The side that went after a DNA test and forced me on the Kingstons. She'd tell me to fight back. She'd tell me to win.

I stand in the dark corner, and I reach in my pocket and pull out a quarter, focusing on walking it through my fingers to calm my mind. Taking myself to that place I went all those years ago when I had to kill or be killed. It was natural then, an instinct that didn't require honing, but I'm not in that place anymore. I'm in the one that came first. The one where my father lives, which makes this not quite as simple as the "kill or be killed" warfare presents. I'll still kill if I have to, but I want answers.

The alleyway is an unmoving box, not even a shadow flickers. I listen for the enemy, and the man behind that dumpster *is* an enemy. Seconds tick by and turn into minutes and he doesn't move, but neither do I. Anyone my father hired worth any salt knows my skill level. Knows I'm here, watching this fool, waiting to act. One of us has to make a move and I decide what the fuck. I'm game. It's been too damn long since I played a game like this one and I find I missed the hell out of it.

I flip the quarter into the center of the alleyway and it lands and then clanks as it wobbles. It's an invitation. Come get me. I wait then and wait some more, but there is no impatience in me. I don't need to move to feel relief. The numbers in my head are running and running for me, calculating risk, assessing my next move. I don't even flinch when the other man must decide he doesn't like his odds, and darts out from behind the trashcan and starts running. Smart man. The odds were against him, but that hasn't changed. I might still be wearing part of a suit, but I'm fast and I run behind him, yanking him back and shoving him against the fence in thirty seconds.

"What were your orders?"

"Fuck you," the man growls.

I smirk. "My mother was good and kind, unwilling to hurt anyone. In many ways, I'm not my mother's son." I knee him and he groans. "I'm my father's son," I add, "and I suspect she knew that when she asked me not to go after the Kingston family. She knew if I did, I'd destroy them. That's who you're working for, right?"

"Fuck you again!" he shouts.

"Again it is," I say, giving him a repeat knee, this time with such force that when I let him go, he crumbles to the ground. He groans and moans, and when a homeless man wanders into the alleyway, I point at him, telling him he's next if he doesn't back off, and he runs away.

My would-be attacker rolls to his back and I press my foot to his crotch. "What were your orders?"

"To scare you."

"We both know that's a lie." I pull up his shirt and eye the gun there, complete with a silencer. "Who sent you to kill me?"

"Your father," he bites out and then tries to spit at me, like a fool. Obviously, my father doesn't know how to hire a good killer, which works for me right about now.

I reach for my phone and snap a photo of him and then grind my foot into his crotch. He screeches and rolls to his side. I grab his wallet. "You're lucky I don't want a mess to clean up tonight. I know who you are. I know how to find you. We'll talk soon. That's a promise." I stand up and start walking.

When I step out of the alleyway, Savage joins me. "I didn't ask for your help," I say, cutting left toward my apartment.

"You didn't need it either," he says. "Which was kind of disappointing. I haven't had a good brawl in like three days." He doesn't wait for a reply. "One of our guys followed you. I caught up. I'm your front line guy until Adam gets here. And there's no interesting movement back in Denver. I just talked to him."

I open the wallet, glance at the name on the ID that reads Joe Melton, and then hand it to Savage. "He was sent to kill me tonight. I took a photo to confirm the identity matches the driver's license. I'll shoot it to Blake since I have his number." We cut across the street.

"Who sent him?"

"My father," I say, "who I'm going to leave squirming in his room, hoping I'm dead for the time being." I pull my phone out to listen to the messages, and the minute I hear Harper's voice, her soft pleas undo me yet again tonight. I go warm the only way her voice can make me warm, and then instantly cold with the certainty that this attack on me confirms that the warehouse attack on her was, in fact, an assassination attempt. We reach my building and I stop to face Savage.

"Find out what you can on the guy who attacked me. Make sure your team knows that I believe we're dealing with hired killers. And I need an hour alone with Harper."

"Understood," he says, giving me a mock salute.

I enter the building, and suddenly, I can't get to Harper soon enough. I will not feel as if she's safe until she's with me. I head for the elevator and dial Grayson to make sure there's nothing I need to know when I get there. The phone rings. And rings. And rings again. I try Mia's phone in hopes that she's with Grayson or at least talked to him. She doesn't answer. My heart starts to race. What if that amateur back there was a distraction and I fell for it? Fuck. Everyone I care about is in my apartment. I start running for the stairs.

CHAPTER TWENTY

Eric

I call Blake on my race up the apartment building stairs. "Get in touch with your man. I need to know my apartment's secure and everyone inside with it."

"Hold on," he says, without asking why.

In the time it takes for him to reply, in the dead space that is my seventeen flights of stairs, I die over and over again. The idea that everyone I love could be in trouble, and that I let it happen, guts me over and over again; a blade for every floor I have to travel to get to them. My mind starts playing a series of numbers. They calculate the odds of me being set-up. The odds of Harper, Grayson, and Mia laying dead right now, which are too high. The odds of them being held captive at gunpoint. The odds that I can save them if they are kidnapped, which are too slim. I don't like any of the numbers. I reject them all. There's a reason Grayson and Mia aren't answering their cells, that the numbers in my head fail to offer me. It doesn't matter that the numbers never fail me.

Blake finally returns to the line. "Eric," he says, his tone grim. "Our man isn't answering."

Those words gut me all over again, as in it feels like I'm literally having my heart pulled from my chest as Blake adds, "Savage is on his way up and I'm sending back-up."

"I'm about to exit to the hallway," I say. "I'm going silent." I disconnect and finish my upward charge and approach my floor, pulling my gun as I do, opening the door a mere crack when I want to explode into the hallway. I scan and find the floor clear, but there's no man from Walker Security standing guard at my door either. Adrenaline and dread swell inside me and I shove open the stairwell door, exploding into the hallway and running until I'm at my door. Once I'm there I pull my key from my pocket and unlock the door. I then aim my gun and kick it open, to enter the foyer.

"Harper!" I shout, moving into the room and finding the living room empty, but no one there with guns or dead bodies either. "Harper! Grayson!"

"Eric!"

At the sound of Harper's voice, it's like an angel singing me out of the hell that the past few minutes have shoved me inside. And when she appears in the doorway that leads to my office, her dark hair in a beautifully disarrayed mess around her shoulders, that swell of emotions inside me from minutes before now includes relief.

"Oh God!" she exclaims, eyeing the gun, stopping in her tracks. "Why do you have a gun? What's happening?" She looks wildly around the room.

It's then that Grayson and Mia exit the office, both in safe condition. "Oh God," Mia gasps, echoing Harper from moments before.

"Oh shit."

That male voice draws my attention back to the office, where a man now stands, holding a gun. A man that I recognize as Smith from Walker Security. "Why the fuck are you not at the door and why is no one answering their phones?" But I know even as I ask the question. My office has crap for service. It always has. It's like a cold spot in a room, haunted for about ten reasons no one but me has ever known.

"My phone didn't ring," Smith replies.

"I asked to talk to him," Harper interjects. "I was desperate to reach you. I was driving everyone crazy. Grayson went and got Smith because he was trying to confirm that Walker had eyes on you to make me feel better."

"Fuck," I grind out, scrubbing my jaw, and lowering my gun, still focused on Smith. "Get an extra man on the door," I snap. I'm agitated, still feeling the effects of fear for what I'd find when I got here. Still feeling that rush of adrenaline.

By the time the gun is in the band at the back of my pants again, Harper is in front of me, wrapping her arms around me. "I was so worried about you," she exclaims. "So incredibly worried."

She doesn't even begin to understand what worried means right now. I cup her head and close my mouth down on hers, and I don't give a shit who's watching. I kiss the fuck out of her, drink her in, drug myself all over with her, and it's a high I can't get enough of. "We need to have that talk I promised you."

"Yes," she whispers. "We do."

"Sounds like our cue to go home," Grayson says.

I shift Harper to my side, but don't let her go. "Keep Walker with you."

Grayson nods in understanding. "Call me."

"I will," I confirm as Mia rushes to Harper and gives her a hug to add, "Call me, too."

Smith and I exchange a look and I lean down and kiss Harper. "I'll be right back." I press my lips to her ear. "Wait for me in the bedroom. Be naked when I get back." I don't wait for a reply. Smith and I fall into step behind

Grayson and Mia and when they exit the apartment, we stay inside the foyer.

"We both know you fucked up," I say. "Don't do it again." I don't wait for a reply. I move on. "I need to know where my father is right now. I need to know who he talks to or who he sees. And somehow, get a bug in his room, even if that means using room service to do it. Just make it happen."

"We're resourceful," Smith assures me. "We'll get it done." He turns and leaves.

I lock the door and stick my gun in a table off the entryway. I have another upstairs. I want this one ready to say hello to anyone at the door that shouldn't be here. Once it's sealed away, I exit the foyer, and walk the path to the stairs, starting the climb; blood rushing in my ears, pulsing through my body, just thinking about touching Harper, holding her again, after thinking I might have lost her. A feeling I never want to experience again.

Harper appears on the second level, at the top of the stairs, waiting on me, still dressed, and looking like she's ready to launch ten questions at me that I don't want to answer right now. I catch her by the waist and walk her backward until we're in my room where I shut the door, and then plant her against it. "You scared the fuck out of me." That swell of emotion is back, pounding at my chest, radiating through my voice. "Don't ever do that to me again."

Her fingers curl around my shirt. "*You* scared *me*. Don't do it—"

I twine my fingers into her hair and drag her mouth to mine. "Don't talk," I order. "Not now. Not Yet." And then I'm kissing her, and she is sweet, so damn sweet. The kind of sweet a Kingston destroys, but I'm not a Kingston. I'm just the bastard son.

CHAPTER TWENTY-ONE

Harper

Eric's mouth comes down on mine, and I can taste his urgency, his hunger. His fear and his need, things I recognize in myself. Every moment that we've been together, has come with someone dividing us, trying to destroy us. Every moment feels like it could be our last. Just knowing that he's here, that he's alive, undoes me, drives me. I don't want to know what he did or didn't do to his father right now. He didn't kill him. He just hates him. And I want to help the pain of that hate go away. He needs that from me and I need him. I need him in a way that I can't even explain. In a way no one has ever made me need, and the honest to God truth is that I've needed him since the moment I met him. And he needs me. I taste it on his tongue. I feel it in the possessive way his hands caress my body and mold me closer. There's a desperation between us, the intensity of the burn we share swelling into an inferno like I've never experienced, like nothing I believe this man lets anyone know he can feel but he lets me know. He takes me with every touch, claims me with every lick, and yet, he denies me more.

He leans back, putting intolerable space between my mouth and his. "I'm not walking away from you again. You know that, right?"

"Am I supposed to object right now?"

125

"You should object," he declares. "You should walk away."

He's a contradiction in this moment, a man who wants me and tells me to leave. "Why would I walk away, Eric?"

"Because you were right. I'm a Kingston. I can't deny that anymore."

I grip his shirt, twisting it in my fingers. "What does that mean?"

"It means I'm many things, Harper, that you won't like, and you shouldn't try to."

I know then that his willingness to embrace his title of bastard is destructive in ways I hadn't seen before. "Because you're the bastard and I'm the princess?"

"Because I'm me, Harper. I always was, and always will be, me."

"I don't know what you think there is to hate in you, what you think will scare me away, but it won't. I'm here. I'm not going anywhere." At least until he shoves me away, which I feel him doing now, even as he holds me close.

His eyes narrow, his scrutiny deep, as intense as the way he'd kissed me, and try as I might, his expression is impossible to read. I search, I probe, and I'm still trying to read him when suddenly he's kissing me again, licking into my mouth, testing my words on his tongue. I sink into him, absorbing his hard body into mine, clinging to him, meeting him stroke for stroke, trying to answer him, trying to show him that I'm here. I'm not going anywhere. He can't scare me away.

There's a low, sexy rumble in his chest that I feel everywhere. It's that moment of no return for him, that moment where he snaps, where he needs to claim and possess, rather than think. He wants me. He doesn't want me to leave. He doesn't want me to walk away. I feel that in him now, but I also feel his torment. He thinks I should leave and no matter what he claims, I think he'll walk away for me. But even as I feel that thought try to build a wall, he lifts me and distracts me.

In a few long strides, he carries me to the bed, a driven man with a purpose and I'm that purpose. But he doesn't lay us down. He settles me on the edge of the mattress just long enough to remove my clothes and then his own shirt, rippling muscles and all that beautiful ink, splashed before my eyes. I'm still drinking in the pure, raw sight of him, before he shackles my legs, and pulls me forward, spreading my legs.

He says nothing.

He speaks with actions.

He drops to his knees and before I even process what he intends, his mouth closes on my sex and then he's suckling, stroking his tongue over me. I pant and try to reach for him, but another lick and I fall backward, letting the soft cushion of the mattress absorb my body, while his fingers slide inside me. I arch into the feel of him stretching me, pumping into me, my fingers closing around the blanket beneath me, and oh God, he's good at this. So very good, his tongue's erotic play tantalizing in all the right ways, too right.

I'm embarrassingly already on edge, already right there in that sweet spot of no return. I tumble over the proverbial ledge, right into a shattering quaking release that says this man owns my pleasure, and while he doesn't know it yet, all of me. He owns all of me. It's a reality that is daunting in this moment of complete vulnerability. He could hurt me. He has that power. And yet he tells me to walk away. Yes. He could hurt me.

He could hurt me in ways that no man in that warehouse could ever hurt me.

If I let myself really love and trust Eric, I'm at his mercy.

No matter where it ends.

I don't like the inevitability of my thoughts and I suddenly need to read his face, to read his emotions, battling my own, but he's already shoving off his pants. Undressing and his cock is jutting between us, thickly veined with arousal. My eyes meet his and the punch of erotic heat between us steals my breath. In another moment, he's laid me back down on the mattress. My arms wrap his neck, and he's on top of me, the heavy weight of his perfect body pressing into me, and I forget what I was worried about, what I needed to see in his face. There is just me and him, and a sudden, intense awareness that we are finally in his bed, where he wanted us.

I forget everything but him. How can I not? He owns me. That was my fear, but I don't feel fear now. No fear at all. But there are other emotions, a swell of unnamed emotions overwhelming me. We're in his territory, his home, the danger and darkness of this night, driving confessions and intimacy to a whole new level. "I'm not just going to fuck you, Harper," Eric promises. "I'm going to make love to you."

Love.

I spoke that word to him, so hearing it on his lips shouldn't send shockwaves through me, but somehow it does. It shouldn't make my chest expand with fear that I didn't feel moments before, but it does. I both want him to love me and fear the moment he does. With love comes real pain when he tells me to walk away and gives me a shove when he doesn't really follow, because he decides the bastard and the princess can't survive.

My walls erect. I need to protect myself. "What happened to fucking the princess and leaving her behind?"

"We just had this conversation. I'm not leaving you again."

"And yet you told me to leave."

"I did," he says. "But I'm a bastard, remember? And not just any bastard. I'm the one who wants you too damn much now to do what's right. You run. I'll run faster. I'll come for you."

Heat rushes up my neck. "Fucking me is safe," I whisper. "Fucking me is—"

"Fucking you is perfect," he says. "And I *will* fuck you, Harper. Every way I can think of and every day, but right now, I'm going to show you more than the bastard. I'm going to make love to you." His lips part mine, his tongue stroking deep, stroking long, exploring, and the demand I'd felt in him when he'd snapped is nowhere to be found. There is just this sultry, sexy, caress of his tongue that seduces me and tears down my walls.

I am his to do with as he pleases. I am his to please or otherwise. I think he really will break my heart. I think he knows it, too, but it's too late to turn back. We're on a path together that must be traveled, no matter where it leads.

LISA RENEE JONES

CHAPTER TWENTY-TWO

Harper

He will hurt me.

But I can't seem to care.

That Eric has literally taken a hammer to every wall I've erected is an indisputable fact. I can't stop him from stealing my heart. He did that years ago, and when he spreads me wide, his hips settling between my thighs, his cock thick and pulsing, about to enter me, I have only a moment of sanity. "We need a condom."

"No," he says. "No, we don't."

"If I get pregnant—"

"Then we'll be pregnant," he says. "Unless that's a problem for you."

It's not.

I won't.

I probably can't.

And if I do—

He slides his cock along my sex, a promise he will soon be inside me where I want him so damn badly, and I'm done with willpower. I don't want to think about what we lost, and fears of what might never be again. I don't want to worry about his father or this family. I just want to be with him. I wrap my arms around his neck. He kisses me and I taste the understanding on his tongue, the passion he feels for me and for us, as he gives me what I want. He presses inside me. My hands go to his shoulders, my hips lifting, asking for more, urging him to drive deeper. I want more, so much more from him, but ultimately it is him who demands more. Him who is taking me to a place of no return. He who already did and I can't deny that truth.

He presses deeper, stretches me and it's sweet bliss, burying his thick shaft inside me, and when he's there, all the way there, he doesn't move. He savors me and us, his forehead finds mine, our breath mingling, emotions expanding between us. Our connection seems to magnify and consume. He consumes me, and in this moment, I have never felt so a part of another person. It's terrifying how much I need this man. I don't know how to feel this intensely a part of someone and still protect myself. I don't know where I begin and he ends anymore.

"Eric?" I whisper and it's a question that I don't even understand myself.

He shifts then, pulling back, the thick line of his cock stroking a path backward, further and further until I arch forward, trying to stop his retreat, desperate in fact, to feel him deep inside me again. He doesn't deny me. He thrusts hard and long. I pant and moan, catching his legs with mine, arching again, and when he cups my ass and angles me, the result is another long, perfect thrust. He begins to pump, and pump, and we are trembling together, kissing, touching, swaying in a seductive dance that consumes me all over again. We consume each other. There is nothing else, and I don't want it to end, but we're both trembling on the edge and I don't want to tumble over. I want this to last and I feel as if he does, too, but there's no stopping this. There's no holding back.

He kisses me and pinches my nipple at the same time and I'm done. My sex clamps down on his cock, and I swear my entire body locks up and then quakes with so much pleasure I can no longer breathe. Eric groans with the intensity of my release and pumps harder, squeezing my ass to pull me against him, and then he's coming, too. I can feel the warm wet heat of his release spill inside me, while the muscles in his back under my hand bunch and pull. And then it's done, we're done, and in the aftermath of a perfect moment, his big body is still holding mine. The implications of "making love" and no condom are in the air between us, while all those emotions I've refused to name ball in my belly and my chest.

Eric shifts us, rolling us to our sides, facing each other, and the wet rush between my legs does nothing to separate us. We lay there, holding each other, words spoken without them ever leaving our mouths. But finally, we both know this can't last, there are people and problems waiting for us. He cups my head, kissing me hard and fast before he says, "There is so much I want to say to you about us, but right now, we need to talk about other things."

His cellphone rings and he grimaces. "Back to the real world, princess." He strokes my cheek and rolls away, and then he's naked and walking around the bed to grab his phone.

I sit up and watch him talking on the phone and my eyes aren't on his incredible body, but rather his face, the hard lines of his jaw, the thin pull of his perfect mouth. He doesn't like what's being said. He's not pleased. "Right," he says. "We'll be down in a few minutes." He disconnects and tosses his phone on the bed. "Let's talk."

"Did something just happen?"

"No," he says, pulling his pants on. "Nothing just happened." But he cuts his stare and the turbulence radiating off of him damn near shakes the walls.

Nothing just happened.

But something happened.

I scoot off the bed and when I hunt for my clothes, Eric's there, fully dressed already except for his shoes, handing them to me, his eyes meeting mine, but there are no answers there for me to find. *Just shadows and pain*, I think. He's hurting. "Your father—?"

"Supposedly hasn't called anyone or communicated with anyone since arriving to his hotel room." That's as much of that "talk" he keeps promising I get before he shuts me down. "Get dressed," he says, and when he would turn away, I grab his arm.

"Eric—"

"He's alive, Harper," he states flatly. "That's what you want to know, right? I didn't kill him." He untangles himself from my grip and steps away, his anger palpable, as is his intent to put space between us.

He's angry and he's angry with me. It's then that I realize that maybe, just maybe, I've hurt him. I've thought him capable of hurting his father when he needed me to have faith in him and his decisions. I do need to get dressed and talk to him, *really* talk to him. I need to make this right.

I quickly dress, and by the time I'm slipping into my heels, he's put his shoes on, too. We come together in the middle of the room and just stand there, staring at each other, seconds ticking by before he drags me to him, his forehead finding mine. "We have to use a condom from now on."

It's not at all what I expect to hear. "What?" I blanch and look up at him, feeling an invisible knife stab my heart. I was right. He's going to hurt me. "I mean—okay."

"Not for the reasons you think." His hands come down on my arms. "I was in the moment with you. I want to live in the moment with you but as I stand here right now, I know that no child should inherit my hell."

"You mean your family?"

"They're only part of my so-called 'gifts,' but yes. My family." His voice vibrates with the same anger I see in his eyes.

"The savant—"

"Is like a monster inside me, Harper. You haven't seen just what it is yet." His hands come down on my shoulders. "It pulls at me. It makes my decisions but I need you to know that while I may do things you won't approve of, I won't do anything I don't think is necessary."

"What does that mean?" I press again. "Your father— "

"Sent someone to meet me in a dark alley tonight."

"What does that mean?" I ask again. "Sent someone— " I can barely ask the question. "To hurt you?"

"Yes. To hurt me."

"No. No. Tell me he didn't do that."

His lips flatten into a hard line. "I wish I could."

"Oh god." My hand settles on my belly, the depth of evil that is this family, almost too much to comprehend. "Thank God you're okay." I grab his shirt then flatten my hands on my his chest, just needing to feel him, to feel him right here, and whole. "What happened? Tell me everything."

"I left the guy he hired holding his balls in pain and came back here but this is war. We can't even think about having a child, let alone a real life together until they stop coming at us. And they won't, which is why I'm going after them. The way I should have a long time ago. The way they came at my mother." Anger and bitterness vibrate through his words and I'm suddenly rocked by the secrets I've kept from him about his mother. Things I've already decided I have to tell him but not now, when those things could be triggers. Not until this is over so I focus on just that. How this ends.

"What are we going to do?" I ask, steeling myself for an answer that I'm certain I won't like but I'm not sure I can reject. Not now. Not after his father sent someone to hurt him, maybe even kill him.

CHAPTER TWENTY-THREE

Harper

"We?" he asks.

"We," I confirm. "I've told you. I'm with you and that man, that man that is your father, is also my mother's husband." My fingers close around his shirt. "I don't want anyone to die but I want this ended. I want *him* ended and there has to be a way that doesn't include murder. So—I ask again. What are we going to do?"

His phone buzzes with a text. "We have people waiting on us downstairs, so right now, we're going downstairs to deal with the houseful of people waiting on us. Nothing more. Nothing less."

I want to push for more but he's already snagged my hand and is guiding me forward. I'm right behind Eric when he starts down the stairs and when he seems to be pulling ahead of me, he abruptly stops walking and faces me, and then his hand is under my hair and he's pulling his mouth to mine. A kiss that is just lips to lips, no tongue, and as we linger there, there is so much to this kiss. There is hunger, pain, torment, and possessiveness. He's telling me that he's not letting me go, and that's everything to me right now. Our lips part and for several beats we linger there, breathing together until he strokes my hair and then laces the fingers of one hand with mine.

That's how we walk down the stairs and when we reach the living room, we find Savage and Blake at the fireplace, flames licking at the glass cover.

"Ho, ho, ho," Savage says, as we join them. "I came back bearing gifts. Or one gift." He motions to Blake. "I brought the hacker extraordinaire. I tried to put a bow on him, but he refused."

"He's not fucking joking," Blake grumbles. "He tried to put a bow on me because he's a crazy person."

Savage's phone buzzes with a message and he glances down at it. "Duty calls. Too bad it's not a woman." He eyes Blake, and they exchange a look before Savage heads for the door while Blake focuses on me.

"You okay?"

"I'm alive," I say. "I'm not bleeding. I'd say that makes me pretty okay. Thank you and your team for all you've done."

"Thank me when I make it count," he says eyeing Eric. "I want to dissect a few dots I've connected, but first things first. You think your father tried to kill you tonight?"

Eric's jaw tenses. "I just covered this. No. I don't."

"Savage told me you did," Blake argues. "That was your gut instinct right after it happened."

"And I'm telling you," Eric states, "it's not now. My father isn't stupid enough to send someone that beneath my skill level to kill me. He knows who I am. He knows *what* I am." His cellphone rings and he pulls it from his pocket. "Speak of the devil himself." His lips press together. "My father." He declines the call.

"You're not going to take it?" I ask.

"Let him wonder what I'm doing right now."

"I don't understand what's happening," I say. "If he wasn't trying to kill you, then why attack you tonight?" I ask. "It makes no sense. That puts us on guard. It keeps me, and us, here. You'd think that they would want me back in Denver with you by my side. That's how they get to me and blame you."

"They don't believe I'll let you go back to Denver," he replies. "Now, they have to do this here. They wanted to be sure I was spooked enough to hold onto you here."

"But how do they get to me or you here?" I challenge, holding out my hands. "We're well insulated."

"Baiting me," I say. "Somehow, someway, he plans to bait me into doing something that backfires."

"Let them try," Blake says. "We'll be there to turn it around on them."

"In other words," Eric replies. "You're not here to tell me that you figured out what's really going on here, are you?"

"Not yet but we need to talk about the unions, and the possibility of them being connected to the Kingstons."

"The unions?" I ask. "You think this relates to them?"

"I do," Blake says. "I can't prove it yet, but I have enough for me to start pointing my research that direction. And believe me, the union's involvement is not good news."

"No, it's not," Eric says, pulling me closer, as if he's suddenly concerned about me standing right here.

I glance at Eric. "What do you two know that I don't know?"

"The unions are still connected to the mob," Eric says. "You piss them off, you die. You steal from them, you suffer before you die. We don't want them coming after you."

Realization hits me and I can feel the color drain from my face. "The money in the account in my name. It could be mob money. It could look like I stole from the mob."

"We handled that," Blake assures me. "There's no connection to you."

139

"That we know of," I say. "We don't know much, it seems to me, right now."

Eric turns me to face him, his hands on my shoulders. "No one is going to hurt you, princess. They'll have to come through me and that won't go well for them."

"I'm not going to cower in fear," I say, thinking of what the Kingstons did to his mother, to him, what they could do to *my* mother. "I'm sick of this family, I'm ready to fight."

CHAPTER TWENTY-FOUR

Harper

I hold onto Eric, but not out of fear. No more fear. My mind is chasing Blake's theory about what's really going on. "It makes sense," I say, facing Eric and Blake. "The union being involved makes sense. Isaac tried to get me to take over the union negotiations last week, right before my attack." I eye Eric. "That meeting you interrupted. That was set-up because of Isaac thrusting a project on me out of nowhere."

"Which, "Eric says, "I agree, fits with them trying to connect you to the union."

"But what could they be doing with the union that involves the kind of cash we know they're moving around?" I ask, looking between both men. "Is it payoffs, and moving the cash around in my name, and even Gigi's, to make us look guilty in case the government catches on?"

"I doubt this is about the government," Eric says. "It's more likely about crossing someone they shouldn't have crossed. Gigi's not innocent. I don't believe that for a minute."

I set aside the argument about Gigi and hug myself with a really bad thought, and a question I don't want to ask, but it has to be asked. "My mother," I say, looking between Eric and Blake. "Is she innocent?"

"Your mother didn't play a part in your attack," Eric promises me. "I wouldn't hide that from you."

"Like your father didn't have you attacked tonight?"

His jaw tenses. "My father and I are not the same as you and your mother. And Adam was there when she met with Gigi. I told you what he overheard that conversation."

"I concur on all points," Blake interjects.

"What about bank accounts in her name?" I ask. "Is she the next fall guy?"

"She has no bank accounts in her name alone," Blake says. "And I'm of the opinion that she's too close to your stepfather to become a target. He wouldn't be insulated from the police."

"That means we stay the target," I say. "I'm some fall guy for something with the union and maybe the mob, and we don't even know what to stop it from happening. This is insanity."

"We don't have any proof that the union or the mob is involved," Blake says. "I'm speculating."

"But you have enough to connect the dots to the union that's working with the mob," I remind him. "You said that. The mob. Does anyone survive the mob if they get angry?"

"Easy, sweetheart," Eric says. "This is all speculation."

"You were attacked tonight, Eric. I was attacked. In two different cities. We need to speculate into facts quickly before someone ends up dead, like us." I face Eric. "Number one," I press. "What's your number one thought right now, in this moment, about why you were attacked? Let the savant in you work. First thing that comes to your mind, now."

"Isaac was scared when he came to your house to see me. Really fucking scared. The kind of scared you are when you've fucked over the mob. And you don't fuck over the mob, or anyone powerful, without a plan to cover your ass."

"We were that plan," I say, following where he's leading.

"Yes, but they can't kill you now," he says. "Not when I'm protecting you. My father didn't come here to kill you. He knows that emotional stress used to set off the savant in me, and become debilitating. I think he came here to trigger me which used to be a lot easier. If he made me breakdown, and need intervention, I'm an easy mark to blame for all their sins. Hell, he might have even hoped I'd kill the guy he sent after me."

"And you could have," Blake says. "He was a former cop, turned PI, with no military background. A poor match for you."

"Exactly," he says. "He doesn't know that I'm not the same person I was before working with in the military. He doesn't know he can't set me off anymore, but I believe he was trying."

"Okay then," I say. "Where does that leave us? When do you actually deal with him and what he did tonight?"

"He needs to simmer," Eric replies. "Waiting makes him nervous, and a nervous man in trouble makes nervous moves."

"And we're watching," Blake says, giving me a wink. "And we're badasses." He lifts his chin at Eric. "Not as badass as your savant right here, but badass enough." He eyes Eric. "Can you walk me out?"

Eric nods and kisses me. "I'll be right back." He starts to move away and I catch his arm.

"Can I use your phone? I need to check my messages, in case they're helpful."

Blake interjects, "Mia brought you a phone that I set-up for you with your regular phone number. It should be in one of the bags she delivered."

I'm surprised and pleased. "Oh. Great. Thank you."

"I told you," he says, giving a wink. "I'm a badass."

Eric's lips curve with the exchange, but the smile doesn't meet his eyes. He's troubled and with good reason. His father's a bastard.

He and Blake start walking away, and I watch their departure, my gaze locked on Eric. He's all loose-legged swagger and confidence, a machine to many, perhaps to the military, who trained the savant in him, but he's also human. Nothing changes that fact. And humans get hurt. It's not a good thought, and the instant the two of them disappear, I hunt down my bags, load up with as many as I can carry, and head toward Eric's bedroom. It takes me two trips to get them all where I want them, inside the master bathroom but once I'm there, I eye the closet in the back of the room and decide that's my spot. I move everything there and sit down on the floor of the giant square room. I start digging until I find the iPhone box. I open it and find it's barely charged. It dies the minute I try to use it. Impatient for my messages, I'm thankful there's a charger and even a plug in the closet. I set the phone up to charge and then start pulling out the contents of the bags.

I find a bag of toiletries and another with a gown and robe. Another with jeans and T-shirts and even a couple of dresses, all with insane price tags that I know Eric covered for me. I don't want his money. I don't want him to ever think I care about that part of his life. I care about him. God, I really do. I glance down and find that my phone has now come to life and it shows no missed calls, but that might be because it's new. Or no one cared enough to call me after my attack.

No one being my mother, but of course, she may not even know about it.

Do I tell her?

I check my messages and find a call not from her, but from my stepfather. I suck in air and let it out. Why is he calling me? I punch the message and let it play on speaker: *Listen to me, Harper. I'm here in the city for you. If anything happens to you, your mother will never forgive me and I love her too much to see her suffer you as a loss. Eric is not a good person. He's dangerous and anything you think you know about what's going on, you don't. Come to my hotel. The Ritz, room 1101. Find a way. I'll be here for twenty-four hours. Come sooner than later. I worry for you every moment you're with him.* The call goes dead and I look up to find Eric leaning against the doorway, his sleeves rolled up, his tattoos exposed. He's wholly male, and he's lethal in every possible way. Of that, I have no doubt.

LISA RENEE JONES

CHAPTER TWENTY-FIVE

Harper

Eric's still standing in the doorway of the closet, staring at me while I'm on the floor, my phone in my hand, that message his father left me is in the air between us. I stand up and while Eric still leans on the doorframe, his body seemingly relaxes, his stance just as relaxed, and his blue eyes are sharp, hard. Intelligent. No. Genius. "What do you want to say to me?" he asks.

"That I hate the Kingston family." His eyes flicker ever so slightly, a hint of torment in their depths as I add, "That I was wrong when I said you're one of them." I cross to stand in front of him, the earthy male scent of him teasing my nostrils and somehow it already represents strength and honesty to me. He straightens, towering over me, and neither of us touch each other, but I want to touch him, and I want him to touch me. I think he wants to touch me, too, but he senses my unease, and he's reacting to it. "You were wrong," I continue, "when you said you were one of them. You aren't one of them. You aren't your father."

"I heard every word of that message."

"I know. And what he said means nothing to me. I'm with you. I've always been with you." I offer him the phone. "If you want to you can listen to it again."

He doesn't immediately take it. He simply stares at me. Seconds tick by and I look down at his watch—black

147

leather, a black face, red hands—and I can almost hear the tick before my gaze lifts to Eric's again. And suddenly he's pulling me to him, his hand sliding under my hair, settling on my neck and then I'm flat against his hard body, our legs aligned, our hips melded together and I can feel the thick pulse of his erection.

"Did you believe what he said to you?"

That he has to ask this cuts me and my jaw hardens. "I can't believe you just asked me that." I try to shove away from him but he holds onto me, an unmoving wall that confines me. I don't want to feel confined anymore and that's what this family has done to me. "Let go, Eric."

"Never," he murmurs, dragging my mouth to his. "That's what you don't understand. I'm not letting go."

"You did let go. And now, asking that question was pushing me away, which is the same thing."

"Just say what I want to hear," he orders.

"I told you that I didn't believe what he said to me."

"Why?"

"*Why?*"

"Yes. That's what I want to hear. Why didn't you believe him?"

"Because I know you, beyond time and reason. Because I know them because of time and reason. And you should believe me for the same reasons."

"I do believe you," he says, no hesitation. "I'm just making sure you do, too."

"I don't know what that means."

"You should," he says, his mouth slanting over mine, his tongue pressing past my lips, the answer I seek, the understanding I need, in this kiss. I sense this. I know this. He's telling me something I don't understand but I want to. I lean into him, meeting him stroke for stroke, my hand on his chest, over his thundering heart.

Thundering with this moment, because of me, but I'm not sure if that's arousal or anger.

Anger.

He's angry, but as his hand slides up my back, and he molds my chest to his chest, I know that anger isn't at me. He's angry at his father. He's furious at him and somehow, someway, I know that he isn't punishing me with his kisses, but rather escaping that message. He didn't listen to it again because, despite his bravado about being a different person now, his father does get to him.

Knowing this, understanding now that he couldn't listen to that message again without taking the edge off, I'm without any reserve or inhibitions. Everything but this man falls away. I don't just kiss him, I devour him, my hands sliding all over his body and in a haze of lust, we're naked, and he's pressing inside me, my back against the wall, his thick cock thrusting, pumping. He devours me in every possible way, but he isn't alone. I'm right there with him, living the moment, feeling the passion. My hands cling to his arms. His hands caress my breasts, his eyes raking over my puckered nipples.

Thrust.

Pump.

Fuck.

If we were making love earlier, we're fucking now, and it's what we both need.

It's wild, hard, and fast, and it's not long before my sex is spasming around his thick cock and he's quaking as he fills me, that condom he claimed we needed nowhere to be found. When it's over, when we're both sated and clinging to each other, Eric lifts me off the wall and walks us into the bathroom. He sets me on the white tile of the counter next to an egg-shaped tub and discreetly presses a towel between my legs that I barely register, but he does.

"So much for using a condom," he says, his hands pressing on the counter on either side of me.

"Don't worry," I say. "I probably can't get pregnant again, but if I did—hey—we'd make beautiful babies together, remember?"

"Babies that inherit my family and my genes," he reminds me.

"Beautiful and smart, like you."

He arches a brow, amusement in his eyes. "Beautiful?"

"Yes." I touch his cheek and then let my fingers trail over his jaguar tattoo. "And strong," I say. "So very strong."

He catches my hand and squeezes his eyes shut, shadows flickering over his handsome face before he pushes off the counter and walks away. I tug a towel around me, while he pulls on his pants and returns with my phone. He stands in front of me and replays the message on speaker:

Listen to me, Harper. I'm here in the city for you. If anything happens to you, your mother will never forgive me and I love her too much to see her suffer you as a loss. Eric is not a good person. He's dangerous and anything you think you know about what's going on, you don't. Come to my hotel. The Ritz, room 1501. Find a way. I'll be here for twenty-four hours. Come sooner than later. I worry for you every moment you're with him.

A muscle in his jaw tics. "What did that message mean to you?"

"That he's the bastard and I really don't understand his endgame, unless he's trying to get me to go back to Denver, where I'm exposed. What does it mean to you?"

He studies me several beats and then to my surprise, he turns away and exits the bathroom. I jump off the counter and ignore my present undress to follow him. I find him at the bedroom window, inky darkness enveloping the city before him, and only then do I realize that he has a mini Rubik's cube in one hand that he's moving around.

The cube that allows him to think, to process. To calm his mind.

Maybe he wants space, but I'm not sure that's really what he needs right now. I walk to my bags, grab a black silk robe, and pull it around me. Once I'm back, I sit on the chair next to Eric and give him his space without allowing him to feel alone. I'm telling him I'm here. I'm not going anywhere.

A good five minutes pass, and then he sits down next to me, dropping the cube to the floor. He's done with it. He's found his answers. "What did your father's message mean to you, Eric?"

"Ten things," he says. "Twenty. Nothing."

I notice the ways he speaks in numbers and I wonder if this will be a pattern. If it tells me his state of mind, but right now, I don't just don't know.

He looks at me, his eyes troubled, flecks of fire in their depths, but it's not fire like he has for me. It's fire like the flames of hell, burning him alive. "If I'm such a damn genius, the man who solves all puzzles, who sees what others don't, why the hell can't I figure out what the hell my father has planned?"

I glance down at his arm, at one of the only words written out in letters, not numbers: *Honesty*. It resonates with me and this moment. Because in this moment, I understand Eric more than I think even Eric understands himself. I know what he thought I'd never figure out, what he doesn't want me to realize. "You can," I say. "You just don't want to."

CHAPTER TWENTY-SIX

Harper

Eric digests my words without movement. We remain on that chair in his bedroom, his eyes probing mine, a sea of blackness outside the window that we ignore. A sea of darkness etched in his heart thanks to this family and his father.

Eric is the one who looks away first, his attention shifting to the window that holds no answers, but then, it doesn't have to offer answers. His mind is where the puzzle of his father's intent is solved. His mind is the genius that can take him, and us, there, if he so chooses. At least that's my belief, that's my gut feeling. Seconds tick by and turn into minutes before his hands come down on my legs and he looks at me, the turbulence of minutes before banked, if not gone.

"Let's eat," he says. "You have to be hungry. I know I am." And with that, he stands up and starts walking.

I don't move. He just shut down our conversation and shut out his father, and maybe me with him. I'm not offended. I assume that he must need time to process his thoughts and I don't know what that means for a savant. I don't know the best way to support that part of him, but it seems that letting his actions guide me until I can have a real conversation with him about it seems smart.

"You coming?"

I twist around to find him standing at the door, peeking back into the room from the hallway. I stand up and face him. "You want me to come?"

"Get your pretty little ass over here, woman. Of course, I want you to come."

Apparently, he doesn't need space, and I round the chair, his hot stare watching my every move, pausing at the store bags to grab the pair of black slippers to match my robe that I remember spying when I grabbed it. Eric doesn't move. He waits for me to close the space between us, lets his gaze slide down my body, and settle on my fluffy feet. I don't know why he makes staring at slippers so damn sexy, but I'm wet again.

It's ridiculous.

He's ridiculously addictive.

He drags me to him and kisses me, heat pooling low in my belly, as he murmurs, "Maybe I'll just eat you again."

I'm officially tingling all over but for once with this man, I have willpower. "Not until you feed me and you. And we talk."

"Hmmm well, we have plenty of time to talk, but food gives me more energy to do all the things I want to do to you." He kisses my hand. "Come on. I'll give you the grand tour, starting with the kitchen."

My stomach growls and we both laugh. "I think starting with the kitchen is a good idea. What time is it anyway?"

He glances at his watch. "Early morning, which means we'll be scavenging food from my fridge and pantry."

"Morning. Wow. How did that happen? And thank God we slept some on the plane though I think I'm running on adrenaline, too."

"We both are. We need to eat and get some sleep."

"Any in TV dinners in the freezer? Because I'm not feeling breakfast food right now and that's what I know how to cook."

"TV dinners, huh?" He laughs as we cross his gorgeous open living area to enter the connected kitchen area. "Well, the good news is that I *don't* have any TV dinners to torture you with."

I stop at the living room side of the island while he rounds it and faces me. "What's wrong with TV dinners?" I ask. "They make healthy, fast meals for one and that works for me. I am, after all, a single, working lady. All I need is a cat to make it perfect."

He presses his hands to the counter, leaning in closer to me, his eyes warm, the turbulence I'd seen in them earlier, thankfully absent, at least for now. "You're not single anymore," he says. "You'll figure that out soon." His gaze lowers to my mouth, a naughty thought playing across his face before he gives me a wink. "I'd better feed you now." He pushes off the island. "How about mac n cheese?"

"Mac n cheese? Yes, please. You have mac n cheese?"

"I always have a good ol' box of Kraft handy." He opens a cabinet and pulls out a box. "Though my mother wouldn't approve. She, unlike me, was a cook and a baker. We lived on Walmart groceries, but she made them taste like Ritz Carlton room service."

"Do you still have any of her recipes?" I ask, warmed by the way his eyes light when he talks about his mother.

"She kept them all in her head." He cuts his stare and returns it. "Perhaps she had a little savant in her, herself."

I feel his mood darkening with her memory, perhaps because that memory is tainted by his father, so I swiftly change the topic. "Well, Mr. Savant, you might know numbers, but can you follow a recipe? We need milk for the mac n cheese. Do you have any?"

"Do I have milk?" he asks incredulously and opens another cabinet with a collection of cereal boxes. "How can you even suggest otherwise? How else would I eat my breakfast that is often also my dinner?"

My gaze traces all his rippling muscles, inked to sexy perfection and I decide that his body is too hot for him to eat mac n cheese and cereal all the time, but I don't say that. I'll just show my appreciation later. "Well then," I volunteer, "let me pretend to have cooking skills and boil the water."

He laughs and it's an easy, masculine laugh that slides under my skin, and seems to settle right there in a portion of my heart, just like the man. I like this side of him, the one that laughs and I think this is what he meant back in Denver when he talked about how different he is here. I see a glimpse of that part of him now. I think he needs the disconnect from the Kingstons right now.

I eagerly join him on the other side of the island to start my pot of water. Once the burner is on, he leans on the counter next to me, his blue eyes filled with mischief. "And you said you don't cook."

I laugh and he kisses me, his mood sobering as he says, "I'm glad you're here."

"Me, too," I whisper, my hand settling on his cheek as he rotates me to face him.

"Harper—"

His cellphone rings from his pants pocket where it's apparently managed to land and he grimaces. "I'll finish that sentence after we eat." He snatches his phone and glances at the number. "Blake." He answer the call, gives a brief greeting, and then starts walking, crossing the living room to stand at the window, which is far enough away to dilute any sound I might hear.

A hint of unease at what could be distrust on his part rumbles through me, but I squash it. He knows he can trust me. I didn't give his father even a moment of credibility when he spoke against Eric. The water boils and I pour in the macaroni, and then the idea that my mother might call has me running upstairs to grab my own phone where it's still sitting on the bathroom cabinet. There are no further messages and I wonder if my mother even knows that I'm gone.

I return to the kitchen and stir the pot, setting my phone on the island. Eric joins me again and I can't seem to look at him or ask a question. He walked away for a reason. He didn't want me to hear that conversation. Eric grabs me and pulls me to him, cupping my face and forcing my gaze to his. "Blake asked me to run a sequence of numbers through my head to see if they matched the messages we were left. Unfortunately, they didn't."

"What numbers?"

"He had the idea that the message tied to union case numbers, but he couldn't make them connect and like I said, I couldn't either."

"Blake's working on that now, this late?"

"He's obsessed with the message and its meaning." He strokes my face. "I needed to step away to do that. I wasn't hiding anything from you."

"I didn't ask."

"I wanted you to know." His voice softens, eyes warming. "I know how loyal you were to me when my father called. It matters, Harper. You matter to me. And just to be clear, I'm falling in love with you, too, and I have no doubt that began the minute I saw you by that pool six years ago. You and that black dress have haunted me ever since."

He's falling in love with me.

I've haunted him, like he's haunted me.

I want to revel in these confessions—I do revel in them—but there's something in his eyes, a dark certainty I can't explain, or understand. And I know that this darkness I sense in him, matters, too, and more than I want it to. It's the Kingston part of him that I told him doesn't exist and now that he's opened the door to it, they will own him and divide us if I let them.

I won't.

The Kingstons will not win.

CHAPTER TWENTY-SEVEN

Eric

The past...

Only half an hour after my father pulls me out of that social worker's office, I'm at the Kingston mansion. He parks in the garage and calls over his shoulder. "Get out."

I want to punch the window. I want to scream. I want to hit him. I don't get out of the car. Meanwhile, my "father" is already walking into the house. I want to turn and leave. Instead, like the puppy dog I am tonight, I relent, and get out of he car. I have no choice. I have nowhere else to go. I close my hand around my mother's note, and glance around the garage, suddenly aware of the collection of three sports cars and several motorcycles, all more expensive, I'm certain, than the trailer I've called home these recent years.

I hate this place already.

"Get in here!" my father grumbles, leaning out into the garage door from inside the house.

I hate him.

He probably thinks I'm planning to steal one of the cars.

I don't want anything from this man.

I cross the garage and enter what turns out to be a stairwell. My father disappears out some door at the top as I start climbing. Once I'm at the door he'd departed, I

159

exit to a foyer and he's not even there. A plump older woman wearing an apron greets me.

"Hello, Eric," she says. "I'm Delia, the housekeeper. I'll show you to your new room." There is grief in her— sadness for me. She knows about my mother.

"Thank you," I say tightly, wondering if the rest of the world feels pity for me. I don't want pity. My mother didn't accept it when she was sick. She'd be ashamed if I accepted it now.

Delia heads up a winding wood-railed stairwell, but she doesn't leave me behind like my father. She waits on me. When I join her, she gives me a warm look. "You can do this. I know you can."

I don't want to ask what she means. I see it in her eyes. She's telling me I can survive because I believe she did at one point as well. Survive what, I don't know, but she survived. I suddenly like this woman and I'm happy to know her.

At the top of the stairs, we turn right and enter a doorway that leads up again. It's a loft room, a place where I'm here, but not a part of this house. This works for me. I have to be here, but I don't want to be a part of this house.

"I'm going to get you some clothes," Delia says as I sit on the plaid-covered bed, with the low part of the ceiling above me. "Are you hungry?"

"No. I'm not."

"I'll bring you food anyway." She turns and leaves, a part of me smiles inside at her stubbornness that reminds me of my mother. I decide right then that my mother sent me Delia. Somehow, someway, from heaven above, my mother is watching me through her. And I believe in heaven, because I can't mathematically prove it doesn't exist, and because she believed in it. Right now, I need her to be there, not in the ground, dead and gone.

Once the door shuts, I pull out the note in my pocket and read a line and another and another: *No matter how hard it is for you, and I know you, it will be monstrously hard, turn your cheek to the insults and attacks. Don't let anyone make you fight. That's not control. Losing your temper because someone else can bait you is weak. You are not weak. Dream big and live big. Use your gifts, don't let them use you anymore than you let anyone bait you into throwing them away.*

Be the man I know you can be.

Not for me.

For you.

I look up and Delia is in the room, and I don't remember her entering. She's hugging me and my cheeks are wet, my heart cold. It's ice that is brittle and breaking.

Harper

The present...

The macaroni starts boiling over as Eric kisses me, both of us laughing as we race to attend to the stove. "So much for my impressive cooking skills," I joke. "Now you know why I microwave TV dinners all the time."

He grabs a strainer and takes over, dumping the water. "A little boiled over water never hurt anyone unless it gets thrown at you." He sets the pan back on the stove. "Believe me, I know." He walks to the fridge and returns with butter and milk. "Now we just need salt and pepper."

"*Believe me, I know*?" I ask, ignoring the food, certain this ties back to his Navy SEAL days, which might be sensitive, but he opened the door for a reason.

He flips his arm over and takes my hand, running it over what feels like welts his tattoos cover. My eyes go wide at what I realize is a scar hidden beneath his ink and my gaze meets his. "Torture?"

"That's pretty much what every day near Isaac was," he says.

I suck in air. "Isaac did this?"

"Yes. Isaac did this."

"How? When? Why?"

"He hated me. We had words while he was boiling water, and you get the idea." He scoots me over and takes the packet of cheese from me. "I got this."

"*He threw the hot water on you*?" I'm outraged. "Tell me I'm misunderstanding."

"You aren't." He mixes everything in the pan. "Bowls are by the stove to the left. Can you grab them?"

"Eric—"

"Let's eat, princess. We'll talk over the gourmet mac n cheese. I'm about to hollow out here."

Hollow out.

For some reason, I get the feeling those words mean more to him than hunger. They mean a lifetime of pain. They mean survival. Eager to talk to him, to understand him, I grab the bowls and a few minutes later, we're upstairs on the chair we were on earlier, the dark night now etched with a hue of orange as the sun rises; almost as if the night has shifted with his mood, because despite his story, despite what his father did to him tonight, he's in a better place right now, and I don't understand it.

"Gourmet," he says, scooping up a bite. "You and me make a good team."

He's right. We do. I set my mac n cheese on a table next to us and turn to face him. "How bad was the burn?"

He takes another bite. "Bad."

"What did you do in return?"

"Screamed bloody murder while our housekeeper Delia called an ambulance."

"How old were you?"

"Sixteen. Six months after I moved in with the Kingstons."

"What did your father do about it?"

"Nothing."

I blanch. I couldn't have heard him right. "What?"

"He was out of the country and it didn't matter. He wanted me to goad Isaac. He wanted me to push his buttons."

"How did you push his buttons that day?"

"A girl and a test that went my way, not his. Basically, by breathing in his space."

"What did you do about the attack?"

"Nothing. I did nothing."

"Why?"

"Because my mother told me that control meant never letting anyone else force me to do anything. And so I never have." He sets his bowl down. "And I'm not going to start now. Why am I telling you all of this? I don't just want you to know me, Harper. I want you to understand me."

"You didn't call your father after the attack in the alleyway because you won't let him control what comes next."

"Exactly—like father, like son, referring to Isaac and my father. When you don't let them goad you, they become driven to get to you, and usually in a careless way."

"So the plan to come here and give them space still might work?"

"I doubt that," he says, "but that's why I need you to understand that I choose my actions based on who I'm dealing with."

His anger when I asked about his father earlier, comes back to me. "I didn't mean to question your character."

"I didn't think you did, but I need you to know that I don't choose my actions rashly or emotionally, or I'd have already done so a long time ago. That's what I'm telling you. Whatever I do next is necessary. It's about you and me surviving. Not them. They don't get to survive. Not this time."

CHAPTER TWENTY-EIGHT

Eric

Harper and I sit there on the oversized chair in my bedroom, bowls of mac n cheese in our hands, with my declaration about doing whatever it takes to ensure we survive what has become a Kingston war, in the air. I wait, expecting her to push back. She sets her bowl down and I do the same and then she grabs my arm and stares at the scar on my arm.

Her gaze lifts to mine. "Anyone who can do this to another human being can kill."

"Yes. They can."

She runs her thumb over a portion of the scar. "They want to end us. You're right. We have to end them."

I arch a brow. "We?"

"Yes. *We.* I don't want you to kill your father, but I meant what I said when we were with Blake. I'm ready to fight."

But she won't have to fight. I'm going to do it for her. I motion to her food. "Eat, princess. Because this tough talk you're doing tonight is making me want you naked and in my bed." I lift my fork. "I like this side of you."

She gives me a small smile and we both take a bite, both turning to the window again to eat in silence. A comfortable silence that I don't remember sharing with anyone but Grayson and my mother. There are no numbers in my head. Right now, there isn't a Kingston in my head. There's just this moment. This woman.

"I was never against fighting back," she says as we both set our bowls aside. "I came to you," she adds, "because I wanted to fight back. I just—I didn't realize how bad things were or how bad they were going to get. I should have gotten my mother out of there a long time ago."

Which brings us to a topic I'd planned to talk to her about. "You can't make your mother's decisions for her. You have to get to a place where you know that no matter what you do, you can lead a horse to water, but you can't make them drink. We can give her an exit strategy, Harper, but she's a grown woman. If she ignores us—"

"I know," she says. "I know. I could tell her they tried to kill me, but I don't think she'll believe me."

"Based on what I saw when she came to your house, no. I don't believe she will."

"She'll think you planted ideas in my head."

That she sees this, despite how much she loves her mother, says a lot of about her and us. "We'll come up with a way to get through to her."

"I hope we can. We're not close anymore. I told myself we were, but the truth is, the longer she's been with your father, the more superficial our relationship has become. Honestly, I resent her and how she's forgotten my father's legacy. Maybe she resents me for pointing that out and I do. Often."

"Did she know about the miscarriage?"

"I didn't tell her, but I regretted that. I feel like maybe Isaac told her. Maybe she knows, and feels hurt that I didn't tell her. Maybe that's why she's so damn angry all the time."

"Who does Isaac think the father was?"

166

"Isaac doesn't have any idea. I don't tell Isaac anything. I damn sure didn't tell him that."

"Were you seeing anyone at the time?"

Her eyes glint hard. "I can't believe you just asked me that." She stands up and I'm right there with her. She tries to walk away. I grab her arm and pull her around to face me but she's already attacking. "I told you I hadn't slept with anyone but you. It was your baby. And for your information, my love life and sex life, have been nothing to brag about which I blame you for. You ruined everyone for me and now you're being a bastard."

"Easy, sweetheart. I wasn't suggesting you were sleeping with anyone but me when you got pregnant. A date is not a fuck. I was suggesting that Isaac might have made an assumption."

"And this has what to do with my mother?"

"I'm just trying to figure out if anyone could have put two and two together. To link us. If anyone could, it would be her. She's the one close to you. Obviously, decisions were made to use me to get to you and you to get to me."

Her voices lifts. "You think my mother was involved? I thought you said—"

"I'm not suggesting she knows what she's involved with, but people use people as sources of information every single day without them knowing it."

"I didn't tell anyone about us—not even Gigi when she asked me to visit you, so it would have had to be someone who saw us together."

"And they could have. Hell, the cottage could have had cameras. We now know that family loves to film everyone and everything."

"I can't believe my mother would know about us that night and not talk to me about it. Honestly, now that I think about it again, I really don't think she'd know about the miscarriage and not talk to me. And I'd like to say that's because she would be worried about me, but the truth is that she's worried about protecting her life with your father."

I see where she's going. She's worried about that ultimate betrayal with her mother. Worried that her mother is one of them, not just blindly in love with my father, and I get that. This family has done nothing but beat me alive. My hands come down on her shoulders. "I know where your head is. Blake and I both told you, she's not involved. Don't go there."

"She's not involved," Harper repeats and breathes out. "God. For a moment there I started convincing myself that she was."

"She's not."

"Do the numbers in your head tell you that?"

"Yes, sweetheart. They do. She's not involved." I stroke her hair. "Let's go to bed and get some rest." I take her hand and lead her toward the bed, and once we're there, I pull the blanket back.

"Shouldn't we be planning what comes next? We're not doing anything else tonight?"

"Just this," I say, untying her robe, caressing it from her shoulders before I peel away my pants and pull her into the bed with me.

She's on her elbow in a heartbeat, facing me, nowhere near winding down. "You're not going to do anything about your father tonight?" she presses.

"No. I'm not."

"Should we use the call he made to me in some way? Maybe I should pretend you're asleep and call him?"

"I told you. We're letting him simmer. And that means we let him wonder if you'll betray me."

She rolls into me, pushing me to my back, her hands on my chest as her stare meets mine. "I will never betray you," she says, suddenly intense. "I need you to know that. Never."

There's a jolt of numbers in my head, emotions pounding at me. "I know that." And I mean it. I just pray like hell when this is over, she doesn't feel that I've betrayed her, and I know, *I know*, that I'm going to have to make some confessions of my own.

CHAPTER TWENTY-NINE

Eric

Harper in my bed.

I focus on just that for the moment. I pull her to me and turn her, her back to my front and wrap myself around her. "I don't know how this ends well," she whispers.

"It already did," I assure her, holding her tighter. "You're here."

Her hand comes down on mine. "I just want to make sure—"

"Don't say anything else," I warn. "For right now, just be here. Don't let that family in right now. Sleep like they don't exist."

She snuggles in closer to me and whispers, "I wish they didn't exist."

I used to, I think, fighting a fade into the past that I know leads to the day my mother killed herself to make me a part of that family. That family is why I met Harper, and I, of all people, know that there is an equation to life and how we all come together and break apart. My mother was dying. That wasn't going to be stopped. I know this now. I've read her records. I've read her words to me over and over, ten million fucking times, and I don't believe the path I took after she left would have changed. She'd set that in motion. She simply sped it up when she killed herself.

The Kingston family was my destiny.

But the problem for them right now is that I'm theirs, too, and the minute they tried to kill Harper, they woke a sleeping beast who will sleep no more. I shut my eyes, but I don't sleep. I think about Harper's assumption that I can't see what my father is planning because I don't want to see it.

When I finally fall asleep, I haven't proven her hypothesis wrong. When I wake up, nothing has changed, but the dim light of a new day has now become bright sunshine that I hope translates to just that: hope. I slip out of bed and shower, dress in jeans and a Kingston Motors T-shirt I kept just to piss myself off here and there when I need motivation to make more money for Bennett Enterprises. I put it on now to think like my father, to sink back into that life. Now it's time for coffee and an empty space that I fill with equations that equal solutions, but I can't leave the bedroom without staring down at Harper, who's snuggling under the blankets.

My woman.

She's mine now, and that means she's mine to protect. That means I'm going downstairs, and I'm thinking us the hell out of this.

Ten minutes later, I have my MacBook open on the island, three Rubik's cubes, and a package of peanut M & M's on the counter while coffee brews. It might not be the breakfast of champions, but it's my thinking process. What I eat. What I drink. What I use to focus.

My lips curve with the understanding I'd come to yesterday.

Focus. That's what my father was trying to do.

Break my focus.

I pick up a cube and start replaying every deal I've ever watched him manipulate. That leads me to analyze all the ways he manipulated me when no else in my life had been able to. And he did. Somehow, at some point, I went from the boy who hated his father to the boy who wanted to live up to his expectations and even please him. It's the one thing Isaac and I had in common. We both wanted to please our father. We competed for his approval. I always saw that need as something that defined Isaac, but objectively it defined me as well. If I hypothesize that it still does, where does that leave me? No. Wrong question. If I hypothesize that it still does, and my father knows this, how would that knowledge create each action he's taken thus far?

Harper

I wake to the warm wicked wonderful scent of Eric and roll over to discover he's gone. I sit up and look around the room to find I'm right. He's gone. I twist around to find the time on the clock on the nightstand and find that it's only ten in the morning. Worried about where Eric is, and what he's doing—about what the Kingston family might push him to do, I throw away the blankets and remind myself that they deserve what they get. And Eric isn't thinking emotionally. He's a man of logic and planning, even with his father.

I pull on my robe and hurry out of the bedroom and to the railing overlooking the lower level of the apartment. I find Eric sitting at the island with a Rubik's cube in his hand and a coffee cup by his side. He's thinking and for a long time, I'm not even sure how long, I just stand there and watch him turn that cube, pop M &

M's, and drink coffee. Over and over he turns the cube. Solves the puzzle. Stops. Eats. Drinks. Repeats. It's an incredible sight that entrances me, not because of how gorgeously male he is while doing it, but because this is a genius at work, and his mind is a gift I don't think he sees as a gift at all.

Eager to join him, but not to disturb his thinking, I return to the bedroom and my God, I stood there an hour and he didn't even know I was there. I grab my bags, head to the shower, and it's not long before I'm dressed in black pants and a black sweater, with my hair flat ironed, and my make-up lightly done. I spray on a jasmine perfume from FRESH I find in one of the bags Mia brought and grab my phone to find a message from my mother. I punch the message and listen: *Your stepfather needs to speak to you. Please call him. I don't understand this new you, but it seems to be the you that stepbrother of yours has created. Please call Jeff and let me know you did.*

My jaw tenses. My stepfather is an asshole, using my mother to get to me. He knows how badly she wants to please him. He knows how badly I want to protect her. It even feels like a threat. Like he'll pull her into this, like she'll no longer be protected. I don't like it. I have to talk to him. It buys us time to figure out what's going on. It buys Eric time to make a move. It buys my mother time to live in the safe oblivion I know will end soon.

I grab my purse, and a black Chanel trench coat, and head down stairs. Eric is now sitting on the couch and he doesn't even seem to know when I enter the room. I set my coat and purse on a chair and stand in front of him. "I wondered when you were going to stop watching me and actually join me."

"You knew I was watching you?"

"Of course, I knew."

"But you let me?"

"You want to know who I am, and me and my Rubik's cubes are one and the same, princess."

He no longer says princess like it's an insult. He says it like he's savoring it and me, that and the warmth in his eyes pretty much melt me and my plans, at least momentarily. He holds out his arm and runs a finger down the only vertical line of numbers on his forearm. "What is this?" he challenges.

I don't know why I think I know the answer, but I do. "How you solve the cubes."

Approval lights his eyes. "Yes. How I solve the cubes, only I no longer see those numbers when I solve it anymore. It's natural, like how trying to please my father became."

"About that. About him. He called my mother. She demanded that I call him. I'm going to see him. I'm going to just talk to him and find out what he wants. Buy some time. And I know you'll say no, but I'm going." I start to walk away.

He catches my arm and stands up, towering over me. "You aren't going to see my father."

"I am. You can't stop me and—"

"I can stop you," he says softly, but his voice is firm. Absolute. "You will not go see my father. End of discussion."

"And if I push back?"

He sits down and takes me with him, handing me a cup of coffee. "I'll fight you and win."

"Calling my mother's a threat. I have to push back. I have to win."

"You win with me."

"I have to go see him."

"No. You will not. I will win this battle with you," he repeats.

I look into his eyes, and I know he means his words. He means to win, but I'm not my mother and he's not his father. "You win only if you give me a reason and a plan that works better than mine, and quickly. The clock is ticking. Threats are in the air."

"All right," he says simply.

"All right? Then what are we going to do?"

He motions to the chess board in front of him. "Play chess."

"What does that mean?"

"I'd rather show you than tell you."

"Eric—"

He leans in and kisses me. "Am I going to have to fuck you into submission?"

"I'm not my mother. I don't submit." It's out before I can stop it and he pulls back, and what I find in his eyes is not what I expect.

CHAPTER THIRTY

Harper

What I see in Eric's face in response to my declaration that I'm not like my mother, that I don't submit, isn't dominance, isn't demand, it's satisfaction. It's tenderness. "Good," he says. "I don't want you to be your mother. And I'm damn sure not my father." He strokes my hair. "But submission is pleasure, sweetheart. The kind of game we play with no clothes on and I promise you, I'll play for pleasure."

"Eric," I whisper at the rawness of this promise, the realness of his man. The *rightness* of this man.

"I wish I could show you, but right now," he winks, "we're going to play chess."

I laugh. "Naked chess?"

"I like that idea, but no. If we do that, I'll forget why we're playing."

"Why are we playing?"

"I'll show you." He kisses me and then releases me.

My gaze lands on his shirt. "Why are you wearing a Kingston shirt?"

"You told me I didn't want to see my father with open eyes. Paraphrasing, of course, but that's the gist of what you said. This morning, I took your words to heart and forced myself to climb out of my head where he loves to play, and get into his head."

He has my full attention. "How does this connect to chess?"

His answer is to offer me his cup of coffee and indicate the chess board in front of me. "Play me."

"Just tell me what you want me to figure out." I sip the warm, sweet beverage that says Eric likes chocolate, and somehow I love him all the more for it. "I'm not playing you." I hand him his cup. "You're a genius."

"Humor me," he says, no denial about his ability to win in his response.

"I don't even know how to play."

"Approach it like checkers."

"Fine." I reach for a piece and make a move.

He moves next. Then me. Then him. I study his position and jump one of his men. "We both know you let me do that."

"What were you thinking with every move?"

My brow furrows. "Well, I wanted to force your next move, leave you nowhere to go but where I wanted you to go."

"Exactly." He stands up and looks down at me. "Think about what happened. Isaac baited me and I left you there at the warehouse, angry. I did what I've done every time with this family. I headed to the airport. I was going to leave. You were attacked. It could have easily looked like I killed you and ran. They set up the reactions, or Isaac did."

"It makes perfect sense."

"But then I showed back up. I saved you. I left with you. I forced them to make a move. And so, my father did. He came here to take control."

"But you're the one in control now. You didn't do anything he wanted."

"What if I did?"

My brow furrows again. "What? I get that I'm not a genius, but—"

"Stop saying that. Stop putting me over here." He motions to himself and then to me. "And you over there. Don't treat me like the bastard."

It's then that I realize that the bastard is more to him than I'd ever imagined. It's the title that makes him an outsider.

"All right," I say, moving on rather than commenting directly, my instinct telling me that's what he wants and needs. "What you just said. That makes no sense, Eric. You didn't go to his room. You didn't call him after the attack."

"What if that's not how it happened at all? He came here to get in my head. He sent a man to attack me, a man who was no match to shake me up, to get into my head. And he called you to do the same." He points to the chess board. "Think about the game. Every move you made was to force my next move. My father took an offensive stand to my defensive position when he responded to our retreat by coming here."

I sit on the edge of the cushion. "So he doesn't want you to retreat. He wants you to engage."

"Unless he doesn't."

"Of course he does," I argue. "He left me a message. He wanted me to respond."

"He was testing your loyalty to me."

"Right," I say. "Of course he was, and hoping I failed."

"There was no pass or fail. Either way, he got to me. Either way, he knew that I'd know he called you. He knows that would distract me or even trigger me into one of my old attacks."

"He still wants to make you the fall guy."

"Or he doesn't," Eric counters.

"Eric," I say, pressing my fingers to my temples. "You're making my head spin." I drop my hands to the cushion. "What's his plan? What's his endgame?"

"To keep my focus on him. That man would not try to kill me and sit at arm's reach where I could just end him. He wouldn't come at me through you, knowing I just saved your life, when he's sitting within arm's reach. Not unless he desperately needed me to stay focused on him."

Understanding fills me. "While he buries something he doesn't want you to find."

"While Isaac buries it. Walker saw my father arrive at the plant after we left. He met with Isaac and was furious with him."

"For letting me live and you get away," I say.

"For digging a grave that wasn't ours. For digging his grave. My father is all about my father. Make no mistake. He's protecting no one but himself."

"Yes, but you retreated. Your history says that you'll leave and wash your hands of them. Why come after you?"

"Because you don't retreat from what you feel is a part of you because of your father, and because you matter to me. He feels like you'll influence what I do next. He needs to influence me, not you. He needs to push me to the point that he knows I'm done with them and then I influence you. I convince you to retreat."

"They don't know we're together."

His lips thin. "They know. They sent you after me. Isaac probably knew the baby was mine. I'm guessing he followed you to my cottage that night. Fucker might have even watched us."

I shiver and hug myself. "I'm back to being creeped out by this family." I shake my head. "But why send me after you at all, if they want you out of this?"

"To frame me and kill you just as we've said, but it backfired. This is plan B." Before I can ask him what plan B means exactly, he grabs his phone and places it on speaker, and in one ring I hear Blake say, "Good fucking morning. You first or me first?"

"My father is trying to draw the attention to himself. He's the distraction. Tell me you found whatever he doesn't want me to find?"

"Not only did we fail," Blake says. "All the little Kingston assholes are tucked into bed in Denver, and showing no signs of movement."

"That coded message. Anything on it?"

"Nothing yet. Today. I will get you the answer today." Eric hangs up on him and turns to the window, crossing the room to stand in front of it.

I waste no time joining him. "If I go to your father—"

"No," he says, turning to face me. "You will not go to him." His tone is absolute, a steel wall, but it's a wall that I have to bust through. I'm the one who can buy time for us to do what we need to do to end this. I'm the one who can make his father feel that he's got the power he craves, the power to distract Eric. I'm the one who has to go stick my hand in a tiger's cage and pray it doesn't get bitten off because I'm the one who won't kill the tiger. You don't come back from murder. I'm not putting Eric in a position yet again to have to remember that. Not when even he sees the way his father pulls his strings.

"I have to do this," I say. "I'm going to do this."

CHAPTER THIRTY-ONE

Harper

"You will not go to see my father." Eric's words are just as hard as moments before, pure steel and determination. A command I pretend doesn't exist.

"I'll let him think that he's bought time to hide his secrets," I say, reaching for the reason I know a man of his genius can't ignore. "I'll call my mother. I'll use her to convince him I really have turned."

Eric pulls me to him, his body as hard as his words. "Now I say to you what I wasn't going to say to you. Plan B could very well be another place and time that you die, and I get blamed."

"I get that. Believe me, that possibility is screaming in my head right now but if I don't go and see him, we drive him to plan C. What is plan C?"

"The same as plan B. Get to me. I'm the bastard who was forced on him and ultimately that he couldn't control. Even you, he chose to bring into his life, through your mother."

"You just said it's likely to kill me again and you get blamed for the murder."

"And then I lose everything." His hand comes down on my head, fingers closing around my hair. "I lose you. I'm locked away where I can't get revenge. I just got smart enough to hold onto you, Harper. I'm not losing you."

I realize now, some part of me, until this moment, didn't believe this man, this brilliant, talented, gorgeous man could feel as intensely about me as I do about him, but he does. I know that he does, and I have no wall with him. I have no way to protect myself, and I don't care. I *don't care.* "And I'm not losing you," I vow.

"Then I need you to trust me, really trust me."

"I do. Didn't me coming to you about the message from my mother tell you that?"

"You tell me that. Tell me now."

"I trust you, Eric."

And then his mouth is closing down on mine, a hard slant, a possession that I feel through every part of me; a lick, a stroke, a command. Yes. It's another command. I will not leave him, it says. He won't let me, he says. And I'm already doing what I said I would not do, submission softening my resolve, weakening my knees, but it doesn't shut down my mind. It doesn't make me forget what I want, and that's him. I pull back, tearing my mouth from his.

"I can't lose you," I repeat. "I won't. Stop trying to make me bend."

"I'm protecting you."

"I'm protecting you," I counter.

"*I* protect *you*," he counters. "That's just how it is."

I laugh. "Really? Did you just take that caveman attitude with me? Because you dictating and controlling me doesn't work for me. That's not the kind of relationship I want to be in. If that's the one you want, you've got the wrong girl. We protect each other or not at all. I'm the way we buy time. With time, you'll figure out the message, just like you figured out your father this morning. You'll take them down. You'll do it right, so once again, I say: You need time that I can buy us."

"*I* need to buy us time."

I push against him, stepping away, my hands slashing through the air. "He gave me twenty-four hours to make contact, and nearly eight are gone. He'll have a move planned when I don't show up."

"He probably has a move already in play and it won't take twenty-four hours for us to find that out. You haven't called him. You haven't called your mother. That tells him that you're talking to me, not them."

"Then I need to call him now."

"What you need to do is listen to me."

"Okay. Then I'm listening. What are you going to do, right now, to distract him?"

"What he doesn't expect. What I never give him."

"Which is what?"

"Me. He wants me, Harper. I already told you that. I'm going to give him me. I'm going to have coffee with my father, up close and personal in his hotel room, in my Kingston Motors shirt. Like fathers and sons should do."

"Not this father and son."

"Today we do."

He turns away and starts to walk.

I plant myself in front of him, hands flattening on the hard muscles of his chest. "So you can walk into a trap and end up dead? I forbid it. I told you. I'm not losing you. How many times do I have to say that?"

He drags me to him again, that spicy dominant scent of him teasing my nostrils and wrapping me in the almighty force that is this man. "Princess, you're not getting rid of me today, or this easily. I told you that if you run, I'll run after you."

"You can't do that if you're dead. I forbid you to do this."

"If you want to forbid me, do it while you're naked. I'll listen a whole lot better."

185

"Fine. Yes. Let's get naked. Am I supposed to complain about getting naked with you?"

"No. You're not."

"Then let's get naked."

"Not now, sweetheart. When I get back." He kisses me, his hand on my head, a deep, passionate kiss, a promise on his tongue that lands on mine. He'll come back. He's not leaving me. With those promises, he parts our lips, and for long moments, seems to just breathe me in before he releases me and turns away. He starts for the door, but no one can keep a promise like that. No one.

I can't let him go.

I won't.

Not without me.

I dart for the door and reach the foyer as he sticks a gun in the back of his pants, and then grabs a jacket from the coatrack. He exits the apartment and I run the rest of the way toward it, open it and jolt, finding Eric standing there, waiting for me. "What are you doing, Harper?"

"Saving you."

His eyes burn with amber flecks, emotions radiating from their depths that I want to know and understand, that I believe one day he'll allow me to understand, if he's alive.

"*Saving you*," I say again, earnestly.

He reaches up and brushes his fingers over my cheek, his touch shivering through me. "You already have, Harper. You just don't know it yet."

I suck in a breath at what is an unexpected confession of which I do not believe this man makes many. His hand falls away. "Walker is watching. They'll stop you again. Don't make them. *Trust me.*"

"Says the man who has my trust, but gives me none by having guards at the door. I'm not a captive."

"Says the man who guards what matters to him and protects what's his to protect."

What's his? Once again he speaks of me like I'm his, and I don't fight those words. I revel in them. I want to crawl inside them and live and love and endure. I want to be his woman. I want to be his everything. I want so much with this man that I can't just let him go.

"What if it's a trap?"

"Traps are puzzles. I excel at puzzles. I need to go. I need to make my move before he makes his next."

"He's driving your moves, remember?"

"Not this one. Of that, I'm certain."

I don't know what that means. "Are you going to kill him?"

He cuts his stare, his expression all hard lines and shadows, his jaw hard before he casts me in an even harder stare that sends chills down my spine. "When my mother died, the *very night* she died, he told me to get over it. People die. I've hated him since that day. I hate myself for ever forgetting that. For ever hungering for his approval."

His words crawl around in my chest, stirring anger at his father, at this family, and leaves me speechless, unable to press for my answer, but he gives it to me anyway. "Am I going to kill him?" he asks. "No. If I kill him, he can't suffer."

It's exactly where Grayson said Eric would land, with a need to punish his father, not kill him.

He brushes a strand of hair from my eyes, tenderness in his touch, that defies the words he's just spoken. "Stay here. We'll go shopping when I get back, after you make good on all of those promises to get naked." He turns and starts walking.

I ignore Smith standing quietly to my left and call after Eric. "I'll be running around your house naked waiting on you, so hurry up. It's cold in this apartment."

He turns around and winks. "I'm officially motivated to hurry back." And then he's walking away again. He's leaving. I shut the door and lock it. He's gone and it feels bad. It feels like he's not coming back.

CHAPTER THIRTY-TWO

Eric

The past...

It's one day until I turn twenty-one. There's days before Christmas. Three weeks before I join Isaac in law school, and I know he's hating that shit. Younger brother tested out of high school, fast-tracked through college, to jump right into law school, years before he can escape my term. Then again, he hates my job at Kingston, my role that grows while he's off turning pages in a book.

Despite my preference to stay at my own place for Christmas and just eat a damn frozen pizza, my father has demanded my presence, so I'm here. I enter the house and I can hear Isaac and my father speaking in muffled tones, too muffled for me to make out the words. And I don't want to make them out. The best days of my life are those where Isaac is gone and so the fuck am I. Every time he comes home, we have issues.

The voices seem to be coming from the den and that's exactly why I head toward the kitchen where Delia will be making the mac n cheese that I love. I make it a few more steps when I hear, "Eric."

At the sound of my father's voice to the left, I halt, and for a moment I fight the wave of darkness inside me. These are the days I hate him all over again. These are the days that I forget our working relationship. I forget our bloodline. I remember the man who told me to "get over" my mother dying.

"Son," he bites out, and I don't like that word. Not most days. Never when Isaac is here. Never on a holiday when my mom is gone.

Nevertheless, I rotate to find him standing in the doorway of his den, only slightly underdressed for a day of fucking with our heads. His dark hair sprinkled with gray, his jaw shaved clean, because that is all that's acceptable. He's in a dinner jacket, a button-down shirt starched as crisply as his spine is stiff, and of course, dress pants.

My jaw is not shaved clean. It's sporting a three-day stubble I embrace. And I'm damn sure dressed like my mother had us dress for every holiday: comfortable in jeans and a blue sweater, because comfortable, she'd said, is how a holiday is supposed to feel.

"Join us for a smoke and the whiskey your brother brought me," my father orders.

I brought him nothing. I figure the games he'll play today are his gift. I start walking in his direction and he disappears into the room.

In too few steps, I enter the den, which by most standards is a welcoming room with walls of books so high a ladder rolls across one wall. Brown leather couches and chairs rest on top of a heavy oriental rug that decorates a dark wooden floor.

Isaac's standing by the fireplace, a smoke in one hand, a glass in the other, and holy fuck, he's dressed like my father. A little clone boy. Clown boy is more like it.

"Celebrating my national chess win," he greets me like it's not been months since we last saw each other, "by kicking father's ass in chess."

"Smoke, son?" my father asks, and the way he emphasizes "son" isn't to ensure Isaac knows that's what

I am. It's to piss him off and it works. His eyes glint hard steel.

"I'll pass on the smoke," I say, walking to the couch that faces Isaac and sitting down.

"Well, have a glass of this fine whiskey your brother brought me. I think it's about ten grand?" He eyes Isaac.

"Fifteen," Isaac says, his chin firm.

"I'll take a glass," I reply and that's the thing about the holidays. I feel my mother's loss. I feel the loss of who I once was. I didn't read my mother's letter for a reason this morning. I didn't want to contain myself. And I don't obviously as I add, "I always like the taste of wasted money, just to make sure I don't forget how smooth stupidity can go down."

"Fucker," Isaac snaps, and motions to the small table by the couches with a chess game set up. "Play. It's better than our conversation."

"Sure you want to do that?" our father asks. "He's a genius."

"I'm a national champion," Isaac bites out. "And no idiot."

Apparently, he is.

Most definitely he is.

My lips quirk and I sit down at the table. My father hands me the expensive whiskey, amusement in his eyes. I down it and set the glass aside. Isaac joins me and sets his smoke in an ashtray, his glass by his side. "You start us off," he says.

No harm in starting things out. I do it. I make my move. He makes his and so it continues, and with every move, I back him into a corner. With every move, I end the game in my favor. When it's done, he stands up and so do I, and he's postured to beat my ass. I arch a brow. He glowers and then turns away, storming from the room.

191

My father steps in front of me. "You taught him something important today. What lesson, Eric?"

"Not to underestimate your opponent."

"No. That's not the lesson."

He turns and walks away.

Present day...

It kills me to leave Harper in my apartment when I want to be there with her, when I want to be naked, rolling around in all her nakedness, showing her how good submission can be. Showing her how safe it can be with me. But I leave her for one reason: the Kingstons killed my mother in ways cancer never succeeded and now they tried to kill Harper, and for that, they have to pay.

The minute she shuts the apartment door, I step up my pace. In about thirty seconds, I round a corner and the elevator opens. Savage is standing inside. "Need a partner in crime?" he queries.

Obviously Smith communicated with his team about my departure but that works for me right about now. "Actually, yes." I join him. "Where's Adam?"

"Oh fuck," he growls. "You SEALs. You think no one is as good as you are." The doors shut. "He's still in Denver. He doesn't trust anyone else to handle what you need handled there. You want me to call another one of our fin-wearing, belly-flopping guys to be back up right now, or do you think you can live with me?"

I arch a brow.

He arches a brow.

"I simply wanted to know if Adam still had eyes on Isaac."

"Oh that," he says dryly. "Yes. He does and he has his lifejacket by his side with his little arm tubes, too, just in case he has to dive in and save someone."

I surprise myself and laugh. "You're a piece of work, Savage."

"And I don't even need fins to swim." He drops that joke and turns serious. "What are we doing?"

"I've decided it's time for me and my father to have a heart-to-heart."

"And he'll expect you and you want me to make sure you don't get stabbed in the back."

"He won't expect me," I say.

He snorts. "No? He sent a guy to try to kill you. I'd be choking out my father if it were me."

I don't comment. He doesn't know my history with my father. Lord only knows, I wish the fuck it wasn't what it is. I wish like hell I hadn't been that man's little bitch, but I have been. I'd solve a million puzzles, read a million work situations and statistics to his favor, but I couldn't read myself with him. Whatever the case, I see me with him now. He wants to buy time. He wants to rattle me, even break me down while he sets me up. He'll have to look me in the eye and try to do it.

Savage and I exit to the lobby and his cellphone rings. He grabs it and answers. "Savage here. What the fuck do you want?" He eyes me and then listens again before he hangs up. "Adam says that Isaac has yet to come out of his house. It's reading off to him. He's going to get a closer look. More soon."

We exit the building, and I've already dismissed Isaac, hiding in his house, like the pussy that he is. That's not reading off to me at all. He's a scared little bitch. He's waiting on daddy to call him with the "all clear" because I'm dealt with. I'm about to be dealt with, all right. I don't voice this to Savage. I'll let Adam confirm Isaac's tucked in bed. I keep tracking forward but a block from the hotel, I stop at a coffee shop. "I'll be right back." I don't wait on Savage to reply.

I walk inside, order two hazelnut lattes, the way my father likes them, two for appearance, one for him, one for me to hold onto, and then wait for my order. When it's done, I exit the coffee shop and hand one of them to Savage. "You can drink what you want of that one, but I need the cup at the hotel."

"You're taking your father coffee?"

"Of course. I want this to be a cordial meeting." I think of the lesson my father was speaking of when we ended that chess game right before I started law school: *Never fight a war as the underdog.* I've let myself act like the underdog with him. I never was.

Which is why I focus on the lesson my mother taught me: *no regrets.*

I pull my phone from my pocket and dial Harper. "Eric!" she exclaims, answering on the first ring. "What's happening?"

I almost smile with her excitement and I would if I wasn't headed to see my father. When the fuck was anyone ever this damn glad to hear my voice. "Nothing yet. I just wanted to say something to you. I know this is early in our relationship, but I fucking love you, woman. Time isn't going to change that. I should have told you in person. I'll tell you when I see you again."

"You love me?"

"Yes. I love you."

"I love you, too, but oh God, why are you saying this now? What are you going to do?"

"Come back, and say that again in person. Naked. Don't put clothes on. Take them off if you have them on. I won't be long." I hang up.

Savage looks at me. "Oh shit. You're going to choke him out."

He smiles.

I don't.

CHAPTER THIRTY-THREE

Harper

Eric loves me? Did he really just say that to me?

Yes. Yes, he did, but I can't let myself get too carried away with this. We feel like we're in love, but we've had six years of being in love with the idea of each other. We're under extraordinary circumstances. I almost died yesterday. He saved my life. There are so many ways we are bonded. *The miscarriage*, I think. Our baby we lost.

We're bonded.

He wanted me to know that now though. God. "What are you about to do, Eric?"

Panic rises inside me and I rush toward the door of his apartment. I open it and as expected, Smith steps in front of me. "Smith," I greet. "Eric went to his father's hotel. He just called and—I think he's going to do something he can't undo. Is someone with him?"

"Savage is with him."

"And Savage will stop him from doing something crazy?"

"Savage is the kind of guy who'll take over."

"Take over? Eric won't let him take over."

"He'll take over," he repeats.

"No. He won't. Eric won't let that happen."

His lips thin. "Savage and Eric get along. He'll take care of him. Eric will be back without an irreparable blemish."

"Irreparable blemish? Are you trying to make me feel better?"

"I don't make promises I can't keep. It's a thing here at Walker. We tell things as they are. We're honest. I can't tell you that they won't end up banged up, but I can assure you they'll end up safe, in one piece, and without any damage that they can't come back from."

"You're killing me."

"No," he says. "I'm protecting you, like Savage is protecting Eric."

"You remember he's a genius, right?"

"Quite clearly."

"He can outsmart Savage," I counter.

"But why would he want to? Savage isn't a man who needs things sugarcoated."

"You're not making this better."

"They'll be back soon."

I sigh and turn away from him, shutting the door again. My cellphone rings where I stupidly left it on the coffee table. I run across the room and grab it to find my mother calling. I hit decline. I can't take it. I'll confront her over my attack and I have no plan after that. I don't know if we want to tell her about all of this or not. I need to talk to Eric first. I stand up and start to pace. I grab my phone and try to call Eric, but he doesn't answer. I repeat three times.

Another ten minutes pass, and my phone rings again, and this time it's Gigi. I don't like the timing, so close to when my mother called. And I don't want to take the call at all. I feel like this woman set me up to be murdered, but I also fear there might be something she says, that if ignored, could become even more dangerous.

I hit the answer button. "Hi, Gigi."

"What is going on?"

"You tell me. Because it sure seems like you know more than I do about everything."

"I know nothing."

"Why is Eric's father here in New York City?" I demand.

"He's—what?"

"Don't tell me you don't know."

"I didn't know. Honey, I didn't know."

"He knew you had me ask Eric to come to Denver. I know he knew."

"He didn't know. Of course, he didn't know. He's furious about Eric showing up."

And yet, Adam says she called him. "Someone tried to kill me last night. Eric saved me."

"What? No. Who? Why? Oh God. Oh God." She sounds panicked. "Oh God."

"Gigi?" I stand up, afraid she's having another heart attack.

"He did know. I'm sorry I lied. I told him after I sent you to get Eric because—it doesn't matter. He knew Eric was coming but—Oh God."

"Gigi, talk to me. Are you okay?"

"I didn't want to see either of you hurt. I don't want that."

She's breathing heavily. Really heavily. "Gigi, I want you to call an ambulance or I will for you."

"No. No. I'm fine. I need to call my son right now. Don't call a damn ambulance. I'm not the one who's about to need medical help." On that feisty note, she hangs up.

I breathe out. What just happened? Who is on whose side?

I could make all kinds of assumptions, but right now, I need to do something more productive. I need to help.

I consider calling Eric again, but talk of Gigi will just piss him off more, and he might really kill someone.

I walk to the door again and of course, Smith greets me again. "Going somewhere?"

"Blake, your boss."

"What about him?"

"He's trying to solve the puzzle from the message we were given. I'd like to help. Can you call him?"

"That I can do." He grabs his phone and dials. A few seconds later, he relays my request and offer, and then hands me the phone.

"Hiya, Harper," Blake says. "You got something for me?"

"No, but I know that world. Maybe I can help and right now, Eric went to see his father, and I'm feeling helpless. I need to help. I need to do something worthwhile. There might be something you pull up that means nothing to you, but something to me."

"Good point. I'll come to you. I'm actually nearby. Give me ten minutes."

"That works." I hesitate. "Blake—"

"He won't do anything stupid."

"How do you know?"

"Because I've looked into his eyes. Because I know that he's stronger than his need for revenge and because he's a genius. I'll be there soon." He disconnects.

I think of Eric's claim that death is too good for his father. He's right. It is. What am I freaking out about? Eric isn't going to let him off that easy. He didn't call me and tell me he loves me because he's about to kill his father. I have a moment of relief and I shut Smith outside, shutting myself inside Eric's apartment. He'll meet with his father. He'll buy us time to end this in a reasonable way. Then we will confess our love while naked and in his bed. The end. That's the ending I choose.

LISA RENEE JONES

CHAPTER THIRTY-FOUR

Eric

Savage sips from the coffee I just handed him. "Your father likes hazelnut latte," he observes. "I would have taken him for more of a black coffee, no cream or sugar kind of guy."

"My father's the kind of man that sweetens his drink and pisses in yours."

"Ah. Gotcha." He downs another swallow. "I'm sweetened up and caffeinated. Ready to fight. What's the plan? Kill him? Punish him? Tickle his feet until he pees himself? Or just piss in his coffee? I can do that right now, if you like?"

"I'd get the honors on all of the above," I say, offering nothing more. My plans are my plans. I don't need anyone else inside them, crawling around and fucking them up. I start walking toward my father's hotel. Savage falls into step with me. "Decision yet to be made, aye?" he asks. "I get it. He's your father, but he sent a hitman to kill you."

He knows as well as I do that that man wasn't sent to kill me. He's looking for answers that I'm not going to give him. "My father has a funny way of showing love."

"Love by way of a hitman. Your family is more fucked up than mine."

He hits about ten nerves with his "love by way of a hitman" comment that shoots me right back into the past. Into the day my mother became her own hitman and shot herself. For me. She did it for me. Because she loved me and I've had a lifetime of fucked-up mixed emotions about her actions that all blast me right into this moment. Into the one where I walk into my father's hotel and head toward the elevator to pay him a "loving" visit.

My cellphone buzzes with a text message and I grab my phone and glance down at a message from Harper. *I talked to Gigi. Please call me.*

I stop walking and eye Savage. "Give me a minute." I step to a vacant seating area to our right and dial Harper.

"What about Gigi?" I say when she answers.

"She called. I didn't want to take the call, but I felt like it might buy more time."

"And?"

"She had a panic attack when I told her I was attacked. Eric, she wasn't acting and she didn't know your father was here. She hung up with me to call him and she was pissed. I'm not misreading this."

"She set us up."

"I'm going to use your own words on you right now. What if she didn't? I know you hate her, but being a bitch and arranging a murder are two wildly different things. What if she was set-up, too?"

"You're suggesting my father used her to get me to Denver, and she played an unwitting role in all of this." It's not a question. I'm simply letting her thoughts calculate in my mind.

"Isn't he the only person that could use her that way? Which means he has to be the mastermind behind the attempt on my life."

It's logical with one flaw, the one that has my father desperate enough to bury the problem I believe Isaac created. That's why he was at the warehouse before he got on a plane and came here, but nowhere in that equation, or any equation I've created, does my father use Gigi to get me to Denver. Gigi is playing Harper and that's not something she will want to hear.

"This changes nothing," I say. "My plan is still my plan."

"And that plan is what? Because I feel like you called me and told me you loved because—"

"Because *I do*, Harper. No other reason."

"Gigi set me on edge. I have a bad feeling in my gut now that I didn't a few minutes ago."

"There is no end to today that doesn't end with you naked in my arms when I tell you I love you again."

"Do it now. Come here and do that with me now."

"Not until I deal with my father and send him back to Denver with time on our watch to end this properly."

"That bad feeling isn't going away."

"Relax, princess," I order softly, willing her to actually take a command for once. "I'll be back soon, but I need to focus. If you need me urgently, call me, but make sure it's urgent. I'll answer."

"Just—hurry.""

"I will." I disconnect and consider the new information Harper has given me, but it changes nothing. In fact, it solidifies my plan.

I rejoin Savage and motion to the elevator. Once we're inside, I eye him, aware that I don't have the room number or a key to get upstairs, but he does. Or he better. I pay his team too damn much to have them be anything but prepared.

"Eleven," Savage says, handing me a keycard. I accept it, put it to use, and pocket it, facing forward.

Savage doesn't ask any further questions. I don't offer any answers or commentary. We arrive at our destination and I cut him a look. "Stay by the elevator."

"You sure about that?"

"Yes." I motion to his cup. "I need that coffee."

He takes another drink and hands it to me. The doors open and I exit the car, and start walking. The hallway is long and my mind counts out the steps without my permission. Ten. Twenty. Fifty-two and I'm at the door. My hands are full. It's a good reason to pause. I haven't seen my father in years. I could do without seeing him now.

I use my foot and knock on the door.

My father answers in a minute. Sixty-one seconds to be exact. "About time," he grumbles appearing in the doorway, his gaze downward turned. "I ordered an hour—"

He looks up and stops speaking, shock sliding over his face. "Eric."

We stare at each other, two bulls in a stand-off over the same red flag and that flag is power. In some way, shape, or form, a play for power has always been between us. Not love. Not friendship. Not father and son. Power. It's always been about power.

Today that power is mine and we both know it.

It was mine the minute I decided to change my routine. The minute I showed up here and faced him instead of walking away.

"You wanted my attention," I say. "You have it and I even brought coffee." I offer him the heavier cup, the one Savage hasn't been drinking from, *his* cup.

He says nothing, but he accepts the coffee and steps back, offering me entry into his suite. I move forward into an elegant living area, with a desk to the right and a television to the left. He motions to a door at the back of the room to the left. I've been in enough Ritz Carlton hotels to know that will be an office where he wants to sit behind a desk and play the power card.

I sit down in a chair, letting him know this is how we're doing this: my way, not his.

He grimaces. "Okay, son. Have it your way." He sits down on the couch, his spine stiff, his tone formal, but he's dressed in his casual gear which for him is a crisp white button-down shirt and dress pants, with his thick head of hair neatly styled.

He glances at the cup in his hand, smirks as if this is a peace offering and he's won a war, before he takes a drink. "Now what?" he challenges and then he's grabbing his throat, gasping. He's starting to choke.

CHAPTER THIRTY-FIVE

Eric

The coffee cup falls from my father's hand and crashes to the floor, splattering with impact, liquid droplets hitting my face and arms. Choking sounds come from his throat, fear etched in the eyes of a man that feels no emotion. A desperate plea for help swims in the depths of that fear, directed at me. I wait to feel remorse. I wait to feel panic over the potential loss of my last living parent. I feel none of those things. In fact, I have several seconds in which I contemplate letting the bastard die and burn in hell. In which I want to tell him: *Everyone dies. Get over it.* Then an image of Harper flashes in my mind, Harper looking up at me with love in her eyes, with expectations that I be better than the man whose blood runs through my veins.

My father falls to his side and starts to jerk, his vomiting a sure sign that he's been poisoned. Aware that there isn't much I can do for him right here and now, besides get him help and make sure his throat remains clear, my jaw clenches and I set my cup down on the table, standing up, and charging to the door. I yank it open to find Savage exactly where I expect him to be, by the door, despite me telling him to stay at the elevator. "Get an ambulance here now," I order, knowing that his team will bypass the millions of questions I don't want to answer right now.

Savage curses and I'm already turning away when I hear him directing his team to order emergency services. I race back inside the room and Savage catches the door as my father rolls off the couch onto the floor, crashing between the couch and the coffee table. I walk to the table, move it and flatten him on his back, kneeling by him to rotate him to his side, pressing his shoulders to the couch and pulling his leg forward. "An ambulance is on the way," I tell him, not so much to comfort him, but out of obligation. He damn sure didn't comfort my mother through her cancer.

I've done what I can do for the man. He's now in a recovery position, a position that prevents him from choking to death, despite all his groaning and panting. Savage kneels beside me and eyes the coffee cup on the floor. "Do I need to get rid of that?" he says, obviously as aware as I am that poison is the culprit in my father's ailment.

"Genius doesn't mean stupid," I snap. "No, you don't fucking need to get rid of the coffee cup."

"Fill me in here, man, and do it like I'm stupid. I'm in this room with you trying to cover your ass."

I settle back on my haunches, my hand on my knee. "He took a drink. He started choking."

"Like I said. Do I need to get rid of the fucking coffee cup?"

"And like *I* said. No, you don't need to get rid of the fucking coffee cup. He started choking in ten seconds."

He frowns, clearly seeing that as a timeline that doesn't connect.

"What you need to do," I add, "is to think beyond the obvious."

His eyes narrow on me and he seems to get the message. He reaches for his weapon and stands up as I do the same, reaching to draw my Glock from the back of my jeans where I put it. I motion Savage to the right, down a hallway to what I believe is the bedroom. I go around the couch to the office, where I find a pot of coffee on the desk, as well as condiments and a half-eaten pastry. I pull my phone from my pocket and shoot photos to prove these items exist.

I don't linger to search the office. Instead, I exit the doorway and cross the living room, traveling down another hallway. There's a bathroom to the right that's clear and untouched. A few feet down, there's a dining room with a conference table as the centerpiece. I walk past it into a small kitchen and check for evidence. I open the refrigerator, but it's empty. I rotate and retrace my steps, returning to the living room as Savage returns from his portion of the search as well, and gives me an "all clear" motion.

The doorbell to the suite rings. Savage and I both put away our weapons and Savage, standing just beside the door, doesn't wait for approval he wouldn't need. He opens the door.

The EMT crew—two men in uniform—rushes in, asking for details even as they kneel beside my father and start administering rescue services. Blake walks in moments after I finish delivering the update. "Join me in the hallway," he orders softly.

I nod but I look at Savage and make sure that Blake can hear. "Office. Pastry. Coffee. Recent. I need to make sure that doesn't disappear."

Savage nods and Blake and I walk to the hallway, stepping to the side of the doorway. "We have about sixty seconds until law enforcement gets here," Blake says, "Talk to me."

"He was poisoned and he's alive because I decided to show up to talk. He's alive because I called the EMTs."

"Did you poison him?"

"If I decided to kill my father, I wouldn't have second thoughts and call the EMTs. I also wouldn't make myself the prime fucking suspect by choice."

His lips thin. "That's not a fucking answer. Give me a direct fucking answer."

"I didn't kill my father."

"Did you try?"

"Had I tried, he'd be dead, Blake. I brought coffee. He drank his own before I got here, along with eating a portion of a pastry, but I can promise you he's not going to test positive for poison."

He narrows his eyes on me, and it's clear that he thinks I just confessed to setting this up. I open my mouth to respond to the assumption, but it's right then that a rush of activity erupts at the end of the hallway, shouts lifting in the air. Blake and I both eye the force of three officers rushing our way and Blake lowers his voice. "This conversation isn't over."

"The one you're having with yourself or the one you're having with me?"

He glowers and we both turn to greet the officers. It's chaos from there, and I answer a few questions before the EMTs exit with my father on a stretcher. "I'll be at the hospital," I tell the lead officer. "You can ask me anything you want there." I don't wait for his approval. I follow the EMT and confirm that my father is indeed stable. Had he been alone at the time of his incident, he'd be dead.

I follow the emergency team into the elevator, standing next to my father, but I don't look at him. I text Davis, not because he's an attorney but because I want to head off bad press for the company and Grayson: *Need you. Meet me at the St. Francis Hospital ASAP. More soon. Can't talk.*

Oh fuck, is his reply. *Need you? What the hell is happening? On my way. Call me if you can before I get there.*

I inhale and stuff my phone back into my pocket, my gaze falling on my father's pale face and I once again wait to feel anything but hate for this man, but I don't. I hate him. If he dies, I won't grieve, but he won't die. Because I, the bastard son that I am, saved his fucking life, by calling for help. But if I find out that he's the one behind the attempt on Harper's life, he'll wake up and wish he'd died today.

CHAPTER THIRTY-SIX

Eric

I start to calculate the who, what, when and why of what happened in that hotel room on the ride down in the elevator, while my father's heartbeat on the monitor pounds a steady beat. He might live. He might die. He was poisoned and organ damage can happen rapidly and fatally. The question is who poisoned him and why?

Nothing about my father being a target makes sense. Who benefits from him dying?

Me because I hate him.

Isaac gets rich.

Harper's mother also gets rich.

I go back to Isaac.

Isaac was scared. He needed a fall guy. Harper and I didn't work out.

Isaac did this, but that means he hired a professional.

The elevator doors open and I eye the EMT to my left. "I'll meet you at the hospital," I say, not about to ride with them. To do so would seem insincere, an actor in a movie of lies, and right now, the last thing I need is more lies.

Nevertheless, I walk with the EMT crew, exiting the building behind them, but the minute I spot the press, I cut into the crowd, dialing Davis as I start the short walk to the hospital. "Where are you now?"

"I just got to the hospital."

"Exit the front and go right. Walk a block down." I eye the corner. "There's a Starbucks." I disconnect. I don't care about making a showing at the hospital. I care about getting to Harper before her mother or the press gets to her, which means I need Davis to do damage control.

I finish the short walk and Davis is there at the same time I am. He meets me at the right side of the Starbucks entrance and buries his hands in the leather jacket he's wearing over a T-shirt and jeans. "What the hell is going on?"

"I went to see my father. He took a drink from the coffee I brought him and started choking. I called an ambulance."

"Holy fuck, man." He scrubs his jaw. "Does Grayson know?"

"No. Go to him. Help him do damage control. Keep this away from Bennett Enterprises."

"That's impossible. You're heading up a bid on an NFL team, Eric. You're high profile right now."

"Just do it. Make it happen."

"You need an attorney, a criminal attorney. Call the guy Grayson was going to use for that big scandal he was in last year."

"*I'm* an attorney," I remind him. "And there's nothing they can charge me with. I'm not going down."

He arches a brow. "You're that sure?"

"Talk to Grayson. Do what you need to do to distance me from the company."

"I thought you weren't going down?"

"Don't push me, asshole."

"You're negotiating the NFL deal right now."

"You just said that. Move on. I saved my father's life. Paint a picture in our favor."

My cellphone rings and I grab it from my pocket and curse. "Fuck. It's Grayson." I answer the line to hear, "I called Reese Summer, that powerhouse attorney—"

I don't ask how he knows what's going on. I know. The Walker crew knows him. They do work for the firm, too. They called him. "Eric?" he presses, when I don't immediately reply.

"I don't need a powerhouse attorney," I say. "That makes it look like I *need* a powerhouse attorney. I'm an attorney. You need to stay away from this," I order, and *it is* an order. "Davis is coming to you. He'll help you do damage control." I hang up and focus on Davis. "Go get him under control."

"He tried to hire that same attorney I suggested, right?" He doesn't wait for an answer. "You do need a powerhouse attorney. You handed your father a drink and he all but keeled over. He might die."

"Go to Grayson," I order.

"I'm going, but we're going to talk about this." He steps forward and pats my shoulder. "Because we're friends and, genius or not, you're being stupid. You're fucked right now, man." With that positive reinforcement, he walks away and Savage, who was obviously following me, steps to my side.

"I have good and bad news," he announces.

"The bad news is your team told Grayson what was going on. What the fuck?"

His lips thin. "I'll get back to you one that. Right now. *This.* We have security footage of a man entering your father's room to deliver the coffee," he says. "No one at the hotel recognizes him. That's good news. It lends to a suspect other than you."

"What's the bad news?"

"He resembles a man we picked up loitering around your building last night."

217

Suddenly my father's poisoning isn't a singular event and everything I reasoned about Harper's attack, I start reasoning in another direction. There was no set-up. I just happened to be there to save Harper's life. I just happened to be there to save my father's life. There's a hit list and Harper's on the list.

I start running.

Harper

Blake never shows up. I pace and wait, but ten minutes turns into twenty and then thirty. I could bug Smith again for help, but I don't. I search Eric's cabinets and find hot chocolate, which I make. I actually really love that he has hot chocolate, and I try to imagine him at the grocery store making the decision to buy that hot chocolate.

I boil some water in the microwave and make the sweet beverage. I even find marshmallows. I sit down at the island in the kitchen with the bag of marshmallows, the cup and drop a handful inside. I snatch a pad of paper and pen I find in a drawer and I start writing the numbers and letters from that sequence we'd been given by the man by my house. I write them over and over, and they feel familiar. I eat half the bag of marshmallows trying to find the memory in my mind. There's a memory. There are also enough marshmallows in my stomach to perhaps make it explode.

I stand up and start to pace, which leads me to the living room. I grab one of the Rubik's cubes Eric uses and start spinning it. What do those numbers and letters mean? What do we deal with all of the time? Parts. VIN numbers. Banks accounts. Badges. I stop walking. A badge. Could it be a badge number? I don't have my computer, but I saw one in the office. I hurry inside and locate the MacBook on top of the wooden desk. I power it up and use my access codes to enter the Kingston system. I pull up the employee badge numbers and type in our mystery sequence of letters and numbers. Nothing. I sigh. Blake checked this of course, anyway. I wasn't going to find anything, but something about this premise of a badge number feels right in my mind.

Frustrated, I decided maybe I'll just ask Smith to nudge Blake. I'm close to something. I feel like if I had his tech expertise with me right now, I could figure this out. I hope. It's worth a try and I have to do something to keep my mind off the fact that Eric is with his father. If I let myself get lost in that thought, I'd picture his father dead right now.

I stand up, exit the living room and head to the door. I open it and oddly, Smith isn't there. A chill runs down my spine. Something feels wrong about this. Something feels very wrong. I shut the door and lean against it. I lock the door, my instincts shouting at me. I dial Eric, but he doesn't answer. Smith had to go to the bathroom. He took a bathroom break. I grab the coat Mia bought me and put it on. My gut is telling me to run and I don't know why. If I open this door and he's not out there, I'm listening to it. I'm leaving. I'll hide. I'll go to the Walker offices. I google their address and find the walk will be short. I have a plan. I'm probably being paranoid, but I can't seem to fight this need to escape.

I open the door again and this time I'm not alone.

CHAPTER THIRTY-SEVEN

Harper

"Eric," I breathe out and any relief I feel is momentary as I take in the hard lines and shadows of his face. "What's happening?"

Eric's hands come down on my shoulders. "Where the hell do you think you're going?" He backs me into the apartment and shuts the door.

He's angry, really angry, which makes me angry. "Smith was missing. You weren't answering your phone."

"Smith was at the end of the hall talking to me. I didn't answer because I was already here."

"And I knew that how?" My fingers grip his jacket. "What is going on?"

"Where were you going?"

"Somewhere safe."

"Because you're not safe here with me?"

I blanch. "What? What are you talking about? *What are you talking about*?" I repeat.

His lashes lower, torment crossing his handsome features.

"Eric, talk to me."

He lowers his forehead to mine. "I can't lose you."

His voice radiates with so much pain that I don't know what's happened, but I know it's bad. He might have killed his father. I think he did. My hand goes to his face. "Is he dead?"

He pulls back to look at me, searching my gaze, his stare probing to the point that I swear he can see straight to my soul, and I hope, I pray, that he finds himself there. Because he is. He's a part of me, all of me, in ways I didn't know were possible. There are so many ways we're bonded beyond time.

He swallows hard and cuts his gaze before he releases me and moves away. I rotate to find him stalking toward the window where he stops, pressing his hands to his hips. A moment later, he's leaning forward, his fists pressed to the glass of the window.

Oh God.

He's dead.

His father is dead.

I swallow hard now and I wait for anger or disdain or darkness to follow, but it doesn't. He told me he would only do what he was forced to do and I believed him. I have to believe him now. Some part of me knows that he needs me to trust him that much. I need the same from him.

I step to his side. He pulls me in front of him, presses me against the glass. "What do you want to say to me?"

"I'm with you. No matter what you say to me, I'm with you."

"No matter what I confess to you right now?"

"No matter what you confess to me right now or ever. Real and unconditional. That's what I want in my life. That's what I want to be for you."

"Harper—"

I wrap my arms around him and press myself close. "No matter what you tell me, I'm here with you. But I need you to trust me the way I'm trusting you. You left because you believed Isaac's lies."

"I came back. We've talked about this."

"But you left, Eric, and just now at the door, you thought I knew what I don't know yet, and you thought I was leaving you. That's not trust in me and us, but I get it. No one in your life has earned that trust." *Not even his mother*, I think. She left him, even if it was to save him.

He cups my head. "I thought you were running." There's a hint of accusation in his tone that he can't seem to bite back. He thought I was done. He thought *we* were done.

"To you. The only place I'm running to is you."

"God, woman," he murmurs, and then his mouth is covering mine, his tongue licking into my mouth, and he doesn't taste tender. Not one little bit. He tastes like raw pain and desperation. He tastes like lust and danger, heartache and need. I sink deeper into the kiss, and this time, I'm the one tangling my fingers into his hair.

He reaches for my hand, covering it with his, tearing his mouth from mine. "You're sure you're with me all the way, Harper? Because it's all or nothing for us. We've proven that. We are that."

"All," I whisper. "I choose all."

"Even if I killed my father?"

I pull back and search his face, sorting through the shadows in his eyes. "You didn't."

He narrows his gaze on me, a flicker of surprise in the depths of his stare. "How can you be sure?"

"I'd know. I'd see it in your eyes. I'd taste it on your kiss. Is he dead?"

"He wasn't when I left him. He's in the hospital and we have to go there."

"What happened?"

"I took him coffee. Playing nice when I knew he wouldn't expect that from me. We were in the living area of his suite, he took a sip, and that was it. He started choking."

223

"Did he have a heart attack?"

"If he did, it was drug-induced."

"How can you be sure?" I press.

"I had plenty of experience with poison in the SEALs. He was poisoned."

"By who?"

"A hitman."

"What?" I blink and air lodges in my throat. "How do you know?"

"There was video footage of a man at my father's hotel door and—here. Walker saw him here."

I take this news like a punch in the gut and I double over and lower my head to Eric's shoulder. "Hitman. We're running from a hitman."

"No," he says, cupping my face and tilting my gaze to his. "He's the one who had better run because I'm coming for him and he's going to tell me who hired him before I kill him."

"Are you sure it's a hitman?"

"Yes."

"Is it Isaac? Is he behind this?"

His lips thin. "He warned me that we were stirring up trouble. So is it him trying to head off that trouble? Or is it the trouble he said we were stirring? Yet to be determined, but at this point, if my father survives, I'd expect him to be on our side and start talking."

"You took him coffee, Eric. The police are going to blame you."

"I'm willing to bet the drug won't show up on any test. Not unless I'm being framed and that's not likely. No one but you knew that I was going to my father's hotel room."

"You saved his life by showing up."

"Yes. I did." His lips thin. "I saved the real bastard of the family, but I considered letting him die."

"Why didn't you?"

"Because I thought of the moment I would have to tell you that I could've saved him and let him die."

"Me?"

"You, Harper. My father owes you, not me, his life. If it were up to me, he'd be rotting in hell right now."

A wave of nausea overcomes me and maybe it's crazy, but I don't feel relief. I feel like I just helped rescue the devil. I feel like whatever that man does from this point forward, it's on me. If he hurts my mother, it's on me. If he hurts Eric, it's on me.

LISA RENEE JONES

CHAPTER THIRTY-EIGHT

Harper

My mother.

That's where my immediate worry settles. I grab Eric's jacket lapels. "My mother. Will the assassin go after my mother?"

"You know I've got her covered. You know I know how important she is to you."

"I know you do," I whisper, aware that he lost his mother, that he knows how much I fear losing mine. "But we're talking about assassins here, Eric. They came at me. They got to your father."

"They won't get to your mother." He presses his hands onto the glass on either side of me. "You have my word."

"The minute she knows your father's in the hospital, she'll come here. She'll come right to the assassin. Maybe that's the plan. Does she know about your father yet? If she does—"

"We won't let your mother come here. And no, she doesn't know yet. I talked to Savage on the way over here. Blake is controlling the flow of information, using their connections to law enforcement to help us. He's talked to the police about the man he caught on film. They know about the safety concerns."

The implications of that kind of intervention washes away any relief I feel over how well Eric has thought through my mother's protection, as the true magnitude of our scenario starts to play out in my mind. "Are we all targets? Is that what's happening? Your father was distracting us while he tried to fix what couldn't be fixed because the union or the mob, or whoever they've pissed off, was already too angry? They now want everyone who is a Kingston dead?"

"That was my first thought," Eric agrees, pushing off the glass to settle his hands on his hips, under his jacket, "but the mob wants to get paid. They don't get paid if we're all dead."

"But the hitman was watching us," I remind him.

"Watching is the operative word. He could have been making sure that he knew where we were to make his move."

"To kill us," I counter.

"To ensure I didn't get in the way again."

"But you did."

"Yes, I did."

"There's no hitlist with the Kingston names on it?" I ask hopefully. "Are you sure?"

"No," he answers, an honest answer I appreciate despite how much it sucks. "But," he adds, "I think there are other more likely possibilities. Like my father was going to share information either Isaac or the mob didn't want shared. Or Isaac needed a fall guy, and since you and I blew his plan to use us, he went after our father."

I gape. "His own father? You think he'd kill his own father?"

He holds out his arm and presses my hand to the bubbled-up marks on his skin. The scars created by the boiling water Isaac poured over him in a fit of jealousy, and just the idea of a man doing that to his brother has me shivering. "He's fucked up," I whisper.

"Yes," Eric murmurs. "He's fucked up. As is this entire family. You know that."

"Too well." It's a truth that stabs me in the heart. I looked the other way too long. I let myself become a target. I can't let my mother become one, too. No matter what that means. No matter how I have to fight back. "What's next?" I ask, anger replacing fear and defeat. "I'm back to, how do we fight back? Because I'm sick and tired of this family turning my life upside down. They took my father's company. They took my mother, by brainwashing her to their side. They took years of my life and they tried to *end* my life. Now they want you, too? No. They don't get to take anything more."

Eric's hands come down on my face. "No. They don't get to take anything more. We're going to fight. We're going to win."

"How?" I repeat. "What's next?"

"We wait and see what Isaac does next."

"And if he does nothing?"

His hands settle on his hips. "A son who does nothing while his father is dying—that is something, not nothing."

His phone buzzes with a text and he snakes his phone from his pocket, glancing at the message and cursing. "Grayson's at the hospital." He shoves his phone back into his pocket. "He's trying to make himself a damn target for the press, the police, and anyone who wants to burn me."

"Isn't the Walker team watching over him?"

"Yes, but that's not the point. He's making their job harder."

"He loves you the way Isaac was supposed to love you, Eric. Of course, he's there. Of course, he doesn't care about being a target. Just like I don't care about anything right now but protecting you and my mother."

"Grayson has an empire to protect and everyone inside that empire that depends on it for their livelihood." He punches in an autodial on his phone and in what can't be more than one ring, he says, "Blake, keep the press away from Grayson." He listens a moment. "No. Not here. I'll come there." He pauses. "Yes. Fuck. I'll bring her." He disconnects. "They called Isaac. Walker still has eyes on him and we need to go to the hospital."

"What was that about bringing me? Blake wants you to bring me with you?"

"Yes. I don't want you in the middle of that mess at the hospital, but he's right. I need you there."

He needs me there. This statement would warm me if something didn't feel off. I open my mouth to press him on that matter when my cellphone rings in my pocket and I remove it to glance down. "Gigi." I look at Eric. "Gigi's calling me."

"Let it go to voicemail. We need to leave."

I nod and shove the phone back inside my pocket. Eric snags my hand and we're at the door in a blink. He yanks it open with Savage and Smith on the other side. "No news," Savage says. "On anything, including your father's condition."

"What about Denver? Anything there?"

"Nothing," Savage says. "All is quiet."

"Then let's get to the hospital," Eric says.

"What about calling Isaac?" I ask. "What do we know about his reaction?"

"Nothing," Eric says, pulling the door shut and locking up. "I'll call him when we're on the road."

A minute later at most, we're moving down the hallway with Savage and Smith front and back. We don't take the elevator either. We head down the stairs and none of us speak during the walk to the lower level, where we exit the building. We exit a side door of the building that I didn't even know existed and there's an SUV waiting on us there.

Eric and I slide into the backseat of the vehicle and Savage climbs behind the wheel with Smith in the passenger seat. We have two men protecting us, despite Eric's skill. I definitely don't feel like anyone is dismissing the threat of the hitman, as Eric seemed to upstairs. What don't I know right now? Because there's something I don't know.

I turn to Eric. "Why did Blake want you to bring me to the hospital?"

"The police have questions for both of us and I'd rather them ask there than at my apartment. Once they're here, they'll start taking liberties."

"Hasn't Blake shown them the footage of the assassin?"

"Yes," he confirms, "but that doesn't erase guilt. It simply offers, for all they know, that he was working with me or us."

Us.

Oh God.

Nerves erupt in my stomach and my hand settles on my belly. "We're suspects." It's not a question.

"Yes. We're suspects."

"But you don't inherit anything from the Kingstons."

"I have no idea what's in the will."

"You might inherit?"

"It would be just like my father to pit me and Isaac against each other, even from the grave."

I swallow hard. I now know why I'm a suspect. "My inheritance. The Kingstons might have borrowed it, but if your father dies, it reverts back to me immediately."

231

CHAPTER THIRTY-NINE

Harper

No sooner do I announce the bombshell about my inheritance than Eric is pulling me around to face him, the leather of the SUV cradling us. His voice low but firm. "Don't turn yourself into a viable suspect or the police will as well. Think about all the people that benefit from my father's death. Isaac. Your mother. Me, perhaps. Who knows who else."

"But I'm the one he took from. Why are you not worried about this?"

"Because it's not that much money, Harper."

"It's millions. It's a lot of money. It's motive. You can't trust me this much. You have to be worried about this."

"You asked for my trust. You have it."

"I do?"

"Yes. You do."

"Thank you." I cup his face. "Thank you, because this, out of all we've faced, is scaring me."

"Motives are everywhere, Harper. I blame him for my mother's death. For all we know he promised to disinherit Isaac after that warehouse incident. They could've fought and my father threw around that threat all the time when I lived with him."

"To you?"

"To Isaac. He told him he'd give it all to me, a good dozen times that I remember. Don't volunteer information and answer with as little as possible. And remember, I offered you a job and a paycheck to rival and exceed what you have now. I offered to make sure you didn't need that trust fund."

Realization hits me. "I can't even go back to Kingston. I don't even *want* to go back." I press my hand to my face and try to catch my breath before looking up at Eric again. "I wish I could talk to my mother and have her really listen." My eyes go wide. "Oh God. My mother. If Isaac knows about your father, she must, too."

"Yes. You need to call her." He releases me and faces forward. "Savage. We need—"

"To make sure Harper's mother stays locked down?" He glances over his shoulder. "We've already talked to Adam about that."

"She's not going to agree," I say. "I know her. She's not going to listen."

"We have a plan," Savage assures us. "Blake's brother, Royce, is calling her as an FBI consultant, which he is, and telling her that she's on lockdown. Adam will show up as one of Royce's employees, which he is, to protect her."

Eric arches a brow my direction. "What do you think? Will it work?"

I nod. "I think it might." I grab my new mini Chanel purse Mia bought me, which I don't even remember bringing with me but clearly, at some point, I did. I even stuck my phone in it. I grab it and stare at the missed calls. "She called," I say. "I didn't hear it ring." I punch the voicemail and play it on speaker: *Your father. I need to talk to you about your father.* I grind my teeth at her calling him my father again and Eric's hands close down on my leg, understanding in the touch, as my mother adds: *Why is he there with you? He's in the hospital. He's—call me. The FBI won't let me leave. Call me now!*

Oh God. They're calling again. I have to go. Just—call me. This is Eric's fault. Somehow it's his fault and you're sleeping with him!

The line goes dead and Savage whispers. "That was some heavy shit." Smith elbows him and Savage growls. "Keep your fucking hands to yourself."

"They're calling again?" I ask, eyeing Eric. "Who are they?" I punch in the call back button for my mother.

"Probably Royce," Savage replies.

"He's right," Eric says. "It's likely Royce."

"Royce is not a they," I say. "I guess she means the FBI." The line rings and rings and goes to voicemail. "She's not answering," I say, feeling panicked now. "Why is she not answering?" I redial.

"I'm calling Adam," Smith says. "He's got eyes on her."

"Don't panic," Savage adds. "She's safe. We have her."

I get voicemail again and look at Eric. "I'm freaking out here."

"Easy, princess," he says, his hands coming down on my shoulders. "She's safe. I'm sure she's safe."

Please let him be right. "Please be right." I look toward the front of the truck. "Smith?!"

"No answer," he says. "Adam must be talking to her. I'll call one of the other men on the ground there."

"And just to complicate this intense moment," Savage interjects, "we're not only at the hospital, we have uniforms at the side door that already spotted us. And for the record, yes, our fuckhead team should have warned us."

"You're not making me feel good about my mother and your team," I say, punching in her number again.

"I have Adam on text," Smith announces, looking back at us. "He's standing with your mother now. She's fighting with him, but he's got her under control."

I breathe out and sink back into the leather seat. "Oh thank God."

"We're about to be in the hot seat with the cops," Savage warns. "Stay where you're at. We'll come around and get you."

"Don't volunteer information," Eric instructs.

"Yes. Okay." He studies me a moment as if weighing my reply and state of mind which is shit right now, before he seems to accept that fact and reaches for the door. I inhale, preparing myself for whatever hell follows, wishing this was just over, but Eric takes my hand and his hand holding mine, his presence, is everything. I'm not alone for the first time in a very long time. Eric has somehow become so much to me in such a short period of time, only really it's not so short. We've been there, in each other's lives, for six years.

Eric helps me out of the SUV, and into the cold night air, I don't want to escape nearly as much as I do this night. Savage takes his position in front of us and Smith behind, which reminds me again of that assassin that I didn't even question Eric about again in the vehicle. I never got the chance. We reach the side entrance of the hospital, some sort of service entrance, and Savage enters the building first. Eric and I join him only to have two police officers step in front of us, crowding Savage and forcing him to step aside.

"Any word on my father?" Eric asks, the question his only greeting to the officers. One mid-fifties with what looks like an oddly fitted toupee on his head and crinkles at his eyes. The other younger, thirties maybe, with curly brown hair.

"He's in ICU," the older man states. "They're running tests, but it appears it might be a heart attack." The man's words drip with accusation, as if the heart attack was a product of Eric's making.

Eric's hand flexes ever so slightly against mine, but his expression is unreadable, unchanged. His tone is steady, unaffected, as he asks, "And the man my security team found on the security footage?"

"We're looking into it," the younger officer announces, his keen eyes falling on our connected hands and then on me. "Perhaps your stepsister might recognize him."

And there it is. The next slap and attack this night has to offer and it's all I can do not to flinch with the first of the many accusations certain to follow.

We're a tabloid party.

The implication that two step-siblings have come together for sex, scandal, and murder.

LISA RENEE JONES

CHAPTER FORTY

Eric

The stepsister comment is getting really fucking old. I don't directly reply to the asshole cop who made it. I don't defend mine and Harper's relationship by reminding him that she's the stepsister I never lived with or even knew until we were adults and years after our parents married. Too often in high-profile cases, and this will be one, law enforcement tries to take the heat off themselves and put it on other people. The incestuous headlines they're already starting to frame would do that—if I let them get away with it.

I drape my arm around Harper's shoulders, making it clear that I won't cower and neither will she. In fact, I plan to make it clear that I'll attack. I glance at the cop's nametag. "You know, Officer Marks. I admire a cop as much as I do my former SEAL teammates," I say dryly, my gaze meeting the gaze of the cop that just goaded us. "Bravery and sacrifice are qualities to admire. Unfortunately, there are those who serve who find power trips feed their egos. Like you, officer. You might inspire me to file a harassment charge and I have to tell you, our firm would enjoy taking on a case against the bad eggs on the force. They put the good cops in danger."

He arches a brow. "Are you threatening me?"

"Quite the opposite. I'm trying to protect the many good men and women you put in harm's way. Now if you'll step aside, I need to go check on my father." I guide Harper around the two men and we've made it all of a few steps, with Savage and Smith framing us, when Officer Marks smarts off again. "Why?" he demands. "Why go check on him at all? Word is that you hate him."

I stop walking and rotate to face both men. "And yet I still saved his life."

"That's still to be determined," Officer Marks says. "He could die."

"Which is why I need to get to talk to the doctors." I turn away and pull Harper closer, kissing her temple as we turn a corner. "Don't freak out," I whisper sensing she's doing that and more. "We had to control them, not the other way around."

"Fuckers," Savage grumbles. "Talk about a couple of bitch cops and I like cops. I like cops a lot. Just not those two assholes."

"Amen to that," the normally silent Smith chimes in. "Amen to that." He points to an elevator and we all pause while he punches the call button.

I turn to Harper and press my hands to her shoulders, lowering my voice. "If this was a professional hit, there will be no poison in his system and this is over, at least from law enforcement's standpoint."

"And if there is?"

"There won't be," I assure her. "Act like you have nothing to fear. You don't and weakness to those cops is like blood to a coyote. It draws them in and makes them attack."

She nods. "Right. Got it. Play the game."

"Play it our way, not theirs. Our way. Own every conversation with them. Got it?"

She inhales and lets it out, calmness sliding over her beautiful face. "Yes." She sounds stronger now. Even stronger as she adds, "No fear."

"No fear, sweetheart. Exactly." The elevator dings and the doors open. "Come on." I lead her into the car, looking forward to the day I can just be with her, minus this damn family. And I'm determined to make that day come sooner rather than later.

Savage and Smith follow us into the car and right before we're sealed inside, the two officers step in front of us, the older one catching the door to keep it open. "Is there a reason you need two bodyguards?" he asks.

"You're assuming they aren't our friends?" Harper asks. "Because we have no friends?"

"Exactly," Savage says. "You think I can't have friends? I'm a good friend." He runs a hand down the scar on his cheek. "Saved a friend's life getting this." He scowls at the officer's hand on the elevator. "Why the fuck are you holding the door?"

Smith pulls his phone from his pocket and holds it up. "Recording. Is there a reason you're holding the elevator door?"

The officer holding said door curses and releases it. The minute we're sealed inside, I lean in close to Harper, my lips by her ear as I whisper, "My hero."

"They're really starting to piss me off." She rotates in my arms. "What happened to reassuring us and protecting us?"

"Exactly," Savage snaps, the giant brooding man himself adding, "We need protecting like everyone else. We have real feelings."

We all laugh and I kiss Harper while the car halts and the doors open. I lean in to Harper's ear again and whisper, "I'll show you how real my feelings are when we finally get home."

She doesn't laugh or smile. She presses her hand to my cheek. "Yes. You will." It's a promise, that isn't about playful flirtation. She's talking about what's going on with my father. She's talking about how real this is about to get. He could be dying. I have to face that and she thinks that's going to be brutal, which means when it's not, she'll think *I'm* brutal. It's not a good thought, but I am who I am, and I've already decided that Harper has to face that reality. A savant and a bastard. That's who I am and with that comes baggage.

We exit to the hallway and Smith and Savage assume guard posts there at the entrance to the floor which is open to a waiting room. Davis, Grayson, and Mia are in that small room and immediately greet us, all wearing casual clothing and worried looks. "He's in ICU," Mia says. "And they won't release further details to us. What's going on?"

Grayson eyes me. "Get an update and then let's talk."

Davis and I exchange a look in which Davis tells me he can't hold Grayson back. He tried. There is no damage control. Grayson won't have it. I look at Grayson again. "The part where I told you to stay out of this—"

"Landed on deaf ears," he replies. "We're friends. You're in this, I'm in this."

"I didn't do this," I tell him. "You need to know that, but the press—"

"Check on your father," he says. "We'll deal with the press later, *together.*"

My lips thin and I eye Savage and Smith. "Protect them. Keep them the hell away from the police and the press." I give the entire group my back, and start walking toward a nurses' station.

Harper is by my side in a flash, her hand on my arm, her steps matching my steps and it feels right. Like she belongs by my side. Like she has always belonged by my side. "Stubborn man," I bite out.

"Stubborn friend," she whispers. "And friends are hard to find."

"Which is why I was trying to protect him."

"Which is why he wants to protect you," she reminds me.

I grunt at that and flag down a nurse who turns out to be an aide who leads us toward ICU. In a few short minutes, she's left to find us a nurse, and we're standing outside a glass-enclosed room where my father lays in a bed and monitors track his breathing and heart rate, which is too slow. "And there he is," Harper whispers, glancing at me. "How do you feel?"

"I don't," I say honestly. "Not a damn thing."

"There you are," a fifty-something nurse with bright red hair greets, stopping beside us. "I heard his son had arrived and wanted an update. I'm Kasey. I'm your father's nurse. He's stable. The police aren't allowing me to offer more details." Someone calls her. "Sorry. I have an emergency. We'll tell you more when we can." Kasey rushes away and leaves us alone again.

"That didn't sound good," Harper says, hushing her voice and stepping closer to me. "I think we need an attorney. A criminal attorney and a good one."

Savage joins us before I can reply and I don't ask how he got back here. He's resourceful. "Interesting update," he says. "Isaac called Gigi and told her about your father, Eric. She immediately rushed to the airport, but she didn't get on a plane to New York City. She got on a plane to Italy. She's running."

Gigi.

The wicked witch herself, but wicked enough to have her own son killed?

243

CHAPTER FORTY-ONE

Harper

Gigi ran? She ran *away* to Europe with her son in the hospital? My hand goes to my neck, the sterile smell of the hospital suffocating me, when moments before it had not. This makes no sense. That woman loves her son. He was the king of the empire that she created. A million thoughts charge through my mind, and I can barely make sense of them. I wonder if this is how Eric feels when he's attacked by numbers, if he reaches for one piece of reason the way I do now.

I turn to face him and focus on that one piece now. "I know you hate her. I know this makes sense to you because of that hate, but it doesn't make sense to me. Why would she run? She didn't order a hit on me or her son. And if she did, which I don't believe she would, running would make her look guilty. It *does* make her look guilty."

"Or afraid. She's running for her life, Harper."

"She thinks she's next. She thinks everyone in the family is going down. She thinks someone is coming for them. Or us. For all of us."

"I'm not convinced we're involved at all. I'm still of the mindset that we were the fall guys for something this family has gotten into."

"You think Isaac and Gigi were the ones setting us up? Not Gigi and your father?"

245

"My father's in a hospital bed. That doesn't spell guilt to me though there's no question, he was here to protecting himself. Maybe that means he was turning on the family. As for Isaac, my first instinct is always to blame that little prick but he has limits. He's not smart enough to plan any of this alone. And I keep going back to the night he came to your house. He warned me to leave before I burned everyone. That's not someone who wants me to stay and take the fall. I know him. He was afraid. He was terrified I'd stir the wrong pot."

My eyes go wide with a memory. "Gigi made a comment about you getting your brains from her."

"Nothing about me came from that woman but the bottom line here is I do believe she knows exactly what's going on. I believe she needed an out for the family and took it. But right now, I need to talk to Davis and get us out of here. I need your help. Talk to Mia. Make her understand how dangerous this is for Grayson. She'll get him out of here. Just get them away from this. Even if it means you leave with them."

"I can't leave. I'm not leaving you, and as you said—if we don't deal with the police, they'll come to us. We need legal counsel."

"I'm an attorney surrounded by attorneys," he argues.

"But you don't want Grayson close to this. A Bennett attorney pulls him in."

"If we need a criminal law expert, outside the firm, we'll get one, but there is nothing to protect ourselves from right now. It's a heart attack."

"They didn't say it was a heart attack."

"They will."

"You don't know that."

He kisses me, a hard press of our mouths. "Trust me." His voice is low, rough, a demand and question all at once that only Eric could make possible. "I'm asking you to trust me to protect you and us. Help me protect the only other people other than you that matter to me. Grayson and Mia."

My heart squeezes with the realization that they are all he has, or they were. He now considers me a part of a small, intimate group of people he allows in his life. "I so need to be right here with you right now, but yes. I trust you and I'll come through for you."

His eyes darken, warm, seem to soften and then harden again. "Go now. I need to know they're out of this."

I press to my toes and kiss him. "I'll ask Mia to have coffee, but Grayson will—"

"Be right by my side. I know. And Davis will be, too, and he, like me, protects Grayson."

"Because he's a friend?" I ask, wondering why he denies Davis that title.

"He's not Grayson." His reply is flat and curiously hard.

I don't know what that means, but I don't push. Not now. I'll understand at some point. "I'll get Mia to help." I turn away and all but walk right into Savage.

"Just a wall hanging out," he says, when I stop dead to avoid blasting into him. "I'll keep him safe while you're gone."

Yes, please, I think, ridiculously relieved to have Savage stay by Eric's side. Eric can take care of himself.

I step around the beast and head toward Mia and Grayson, who are standing in a waiting area just around a corner, and in deep conversation with Davis. "What's happening?" Mia asks the minute they spy my approach.

"He's stable," I say, joining them. "That's all they'll tell us."

Davis discreetly steps away, headed toward the ICU, but Grayson fixes his attention on me. "How much trouble is he in?"

"He didn't do this," I say. "I'm certain of it."

"Who did?"

"I'll let Eric share his theories on that," I say, "but Grayson, as long as you're here, he won't think his way out of this."

"As long as I'm here, he'll be forced to think beyond his damn family, and find a way out."

My brow furrows. "I don't understand."

"When a Kingston is involved, that brain of his goes swimming in shark-infested waters where any productive thought dies. He needs reasons to think outside those waters. That's me and that's you. You'll stay close to him and so will I." He starts to walk away to follow Davis, and I catch his arm.

"Wait." He turns to look at me. "His thoughts aren't the only thing that goes swimming in those shark-infested waters. If you force his hand, if you put yourself in harm's way, he'll find a way to end this and I'm not sure either of us want to know where that leads him. You don't know—"

His jaw clamps down. "I might not know the entire situation, but I do know him. I know him far better than you think I know him. He won't go to that dark place when I'm with him. He won't go there when you're with him either. Keep him close. I damn sure am."

"You said he was fine at the apartment."

"His father wasn't lying in a hospital bed, either." He pulls away from me and starts walking, and it's clear to me that Grayson does know Eric. He knows a dark side of Eric that I have sensed, but rejected. He knows that side of him to the point that he doesn't want to let him out of his sight or mine.

"Coffee?" Mia suggests.

I force myself to turn to her. "Yes," I say, battling a need to go to Eric, but remembering my commitment to him as well, to use Mia to get Grayson out of here, though I'm not certain that's smart right now. I manage a weak smile. "Coffee is good."

"I know where the coffee shop is. I was here for a client's mother a while back."

I don't move. I don't want the coffee. Damn it, I have to talk to her. "Great," I say. "Lead the way."

"Of course," she says and we start walking, but suddenly I just know Eric is near. I stop and turn to find he, Davis, and Grayson, entering the waiting room we just left. They huddle up and start talking and as if he senses me looking at him, his attention shifts, and suddenly I'm captured in his intense stare.

Seconds tick by and I can't explain it, but the world just shuts down, it shrinks, and pulls us together. There is so much between me and this man, so much to learn, to know, to experience. So much to lose and I have a horrible feeling that's where this is headed.

Pain.

Loss.

Goodbye.

I need to do something I'm not doing.

What? What do I need to do that I'm not doing?

CHAPTER FORTY-TWO

Harper

Eric and I are still staring at each other from across the hospital hallway with the world fading into the distance. Eric's eyes narrow on me, a question in their depths and apparently he doesn't like the answer he finds in mine because he starts walking toward me. I don't know what he saw in me but suddenly, I just need his arms around me. I need to feel him close and I start running toward him. If he's swimming in shark-infested waters as Grayson proclaimed, I'm right there with him.

I hurry forward, closing the space between me and him before we collide and my arms wrap around him, my head resting on the solid wall of his chest. He holds me close, and for seconds, I wish could be hours, there is nothing but me and him. No Kingston family. No hospital. No assassin, but the world screams around us, and we pull back in unison to look at each other. "We will get to the other side of this," he promises.

"I know," I say, realizing that that's what I need to say to him. "I know we will. I really need you. You know that, right?"

He cups my head and kisses me, a deep stroke of tongue before he says, "Remember that. You need to remember that."

"What does that mean?"

251

"It means we need to be alone. We need to sleep. We need to finally talk, *really* talk." He strokes my cheek. "Go do what you need to do. Let's get out of here sooner than later."

I want to push for more, but he's right. We need to get out of this hospital. And so I nod and step back from him, our fingers catching, and slowly parting, but I say nothing else. He says nothing else. We don't need to say more. What we need is to be alone. We're new. We're unsteady and the world around us is even more unsteady, and we have to steady it together.

I force myself to turn away, and rejoin Mia, and the two of us fall into step together, and round a corner that leads us toward an elevator. A few minutes later, we're sitting in a desolate cafeteria at a tiny table, with coffee in front of us, her keen eyes on my face. "He really matters to you."

"He really does. And that's why I'm going to get right to the point. Grayson's right. Eric is swimming in shark-infested waters, and while Grayson feels he needs to be with him to protect him, I believe that any risk or backlash against you or Grayson is what will send Eric over the edge."

"Define over the edge."

"He'll protect you and Grayson at all costs. He needs room to breathe. If Grayson's by his side, he won't breathe. He'll feel the pressure to end this before Grayson gets in too deep. And I mean, end it however he has to end it."

She sits back, looking as if she were punched in the chest before she leans forward. "However he has to end it?"

"Yes. However, he has to end it."

She lifts a hand. "I'm not going to try to define what you might be implying. The bottom line is that Grayson loves Eric like a brother. He doesn't want Eric to feel alone. He won't leave his side."

"Eric doesn't feel alone. He knows he has Grayson. He speaks of him as blood, family. A brother. He can't lose him. That's what Grayson needs to understand. Eric can't lose him. He can't be a part of taking him down in some way. And you need to understand how dangerous this is, Mia. They tried to kill me and we don't know who they even are. Now his father was poisoned. Eric has every reason to believe that danger is a living, breathing monster, ready to attack at any moment. He won't sit back and let Grayson get hurt."

"What do you want me to do?"

"Get Grayson out of here. Even if it's just for now. I know Grayson feels that he needs to be here but now, now is not the time. He's putting himself on the wrong radars and that's putting Eric on edge. Please. I beg of you. Pull him back."

"I don't know if I can," she proclaims solemnly.

"Try. Please."

"I will. Yes. Of course, I will. I want everyone safe. I want everyone past whatever this is, but I know him. Give him a few minutes with Eric to feel good about where Eric is mentally right now, and then I'll get him out of here, somehow, someway." She tilts her head and studies me. "In the meantime, let's talk about you. They tried to kill you. Your world is shaken to the core. How are you?"

"I'm okay if Eric and my mother are okay. That's the bottom line for me."

"You were attacked. You're going to have to slow down and think about you at some point or the reality of it is going to sideswipe you. You're going to have to deal emotionally with your attack, but for now, I get it. You've banked it. You've put it in a place and buried it because you care about other people. Because it's survival."

LISA RENEE JONES

"I feel fine. I do. I'm fine."

She gives me a keen look. "Are you convincing you or me?"

"I'm fine," I repeat firmly, and I am. I have to be.

"How's your mother handling things? Is she coming here?"

"God, no. We're not letting her come here if we can help it, and she's not a friend to Eric. He doesn't need that right now."

"Is that a problem for you two?"

"No, it's not. My mother needs to open her eyes and see that Eric is the one helping her, not the opposite."

"Sounds like we need to sit down with wine rather than coffee."

"Well, wine would be good, but I can't afford to be anything but sharp right now. Please. Get Grayson out of here."

"Okay. I'll go, but I need to ask you something. I need you to be honest." She leans in closer again and lowers her voice. "Did Eric do this?"

I hate that she's asking me this again. I hate that her doubt reflects Grayson's doubt. It hits me then that maybe, just maybe, Grayson's shift in position on Eric, is him seeing Eric and what's happened today with too much reflection on their youth. "I already answered that question. No." My tone is firm and absolute. "No, he did not do this."

"That was a fast and sure answer."

"And an honest one."

"I like real and honest." Her eyes soften the way her voice did moments before. "You're good for him. He's different with you, not so shut off and reserved. That's how I'll get Grayson to step back. Eric has you and you're his Mia." She stands up. "You coming back with me?"

"I'm going to get Eric a coffee and then I'll be there."

254

She nods and when I stand she hugs me. "You're family now, too. If you need me, I'm here for you." With that, she's gone, hurrying toward the cafeteria exit, and disappearing into the hallway.

I walk to the register and pay for another cup off coffee. With my cup and an empty cup in hand, I head toward the coffee bar and and prepare a fresh cup for me and a new cup for Eric, doctoring his the way I've already noted he prefers. I've just finished up, both hot coffees in hand, when I turn to find a tall, muscular man with a salt and pepper beard standing in front of me, or more like towering over me. I jolt to a halt, all but toe to toe with him. His lips curve, a hint of evil in that barely-there smirk. "It's way past time that you and I have a talk, Harper."

CHAPTER FORTY-THREE

Eric

Grayson, Davis, and I are standing in the waiting room when Grayson's phone rings. He grabs his phone from his pocket and glances at the caller ID. "It's our friendly investor who stabbed us in the back over the NFL deal." He hits the decline button. "I'll talk to him tomorrow."

The NFL deal that represents the dream Grayson and I have shared for years: owning part of a team. It's our pet project together and yet I haven't thought about it in twenty-four hours. "I promised you that I'll handle it tomorrow," I say. "I will. We won't lose this deal. You have my word."

Grayson's hand comes down on my shoulder. "We're a good team. I can carry some of the weight right now."

Davis chooses then to chime in. "I need to speak to Eric. Alone."

Grayson arches an amused brow. "At least you plot against me behind my back, openly and honestly." He chuckles, a man confident enough to know when to step away and fear nothing. And with that, he simply walks away and leaves me with Davis.

"I don't want this hell I'm living to stain the firm," I say, the minute he's out of hearing range. "I need you to distance him from me right now."

"NFL," he says. "We're negotiating the purchase of an *NFL team. You're* negotiating the purchase of an NFL team. That's un-fucking-believable. It's damn near a wet dream. You did this, Eric. You made it happen. I can only do so much in these circumstances, but that said, I'll do everything I can."

"I'm not coming to the office. That'll bring the press to the doorstep of the company."

"We're going to get press. We get lots of bad press. Many times and many ways, outside of this situation. Don't assume our weakness. We have always managed to come out on top just fine."

"This is different."

"The difference is that you're acting like a little bitch, running scared."

My jaw sets hard. "Don't push me, Davis."

"Don't make me. I say own the fuck out of this. Don't walk away. Don't stay away. That makes you, and us, look like there's something to hide. And we don't even know if this is an issue yet. There's no charge. There's no problem."

"There's a fucking assassin on the loose. That's a problem. They went after my woman. They went after my father. What happens when they go after Grayson? I don't need him to be on the radar of the wrong people."

He blanches. "An assassin?"

"Yes, Davis. I don't have time to give you the details right now, but I need Grayson and Mia out of this."

"Do I want to know the details?"

"No. Don't ask."

A muscle in his jaw tics. He wants to push for more but seems to think better of it, at least for now. "I'll find a way to get them out of the city without them connecting the dots to you, but that means I need to use the NFL deal to make it happen. You have to step back."

"Meaning what?"

"If Grayson thinks there's a targeted meeting for that project, and that he's handling it for you, he'll go."

He's right. The NFL deal is the only way to get Grayson out of here. "I can make that happen. I'll make a few calls. You press him to take over. Tell him you think I'm too distracted. Be an asshole. You're good at it."

He smirks. "Yes, friend. I'll be an asshole, just for you."

Mia joins us then. "Where's Grayson?"

"Where's Harper?" I counter.

"She's grabbing you coffee and—"

"She's alone?"

"Yes, but—"

"Safety in numbers, Mia," I say, and I'm already walking. Fuck. I have a bad feeling right now. Why did I let her and Mia go anywhere without protection? Why did I discount an ICU floor as a danger zone? My heart thunders in my ears, numbers pounding at my mind, calculating the odds that Harper is in danger, but the numbers aren't what sets me off. It's a gut instinct that tells me she's in trouble.

I start to jog toward the cafeteria.

Harper

In the seconds after the bearded man steps in front of me, time seems to stand still. What is seconds, maybe a minute, tick by like an hour. Adrenaline pumps through me and I want to run. I want to scream.

259

Is he here to kill me?

Is he the assassin that put Eric's father in the hospital?

I force myself to inhale deeply and reach deep to a lesson that my father taught me about calming myself and making rational decisions. I ground myself by focusing on the mundane details around me, rather than my death. The first thought I have is that the cafeteria smells of pizza. The man in front of me like coffee, the way I smell when I sit in a Starbucks for hours to catch up on work. These random observations work, as they always did in my professional life. My pulse steadies. My gaze sharpens on the man.

"Who are you?"

"Let's sit down and talk," he replies, and it's not a question. It's an order.

Now that he's spoken again, I'm hyper-focused on him, just him, and I drink in every detail I can. The fine lines by his eyes aging him to early forties. His beard neatly trimmed. His cheekbones high, a scar across the right side of his face. His eyes a teal blue. He towers over me a good twelve inches. He's in a black designer leather jacket, wearing black jeans. I don't know what's on his feet because I'm not looking down and giving him the chance to come at me. Voices sound to the left, and the tension in my spine eases ever so slightly. He can't kill me here. And would an assassin walk up to me like this?

No.

That's illogical.

Isn't it?

"Who are you and what do you want?" I ask, wishing like hell the coffee cups in my hands didn't have lids on them.

"Excuse me," a female voice says to my left. "Do you mind if I grab a napkin?"

I'm standing in front of the condiments and supply area. It's a good public place to be but I can't block the path to others using the area. I step slightly to the right, in front of the creamer, giving the woman room to grab her napkin, but I don't look at her. I'm not leaving our public location. I'm not giving him a chance to grab me.

The woman moves closer and she messes with the napkins and doesn't seem in a hurry to leave. It's odd and I have this sense that she's listening in, that she's intentionally crowding us but I'm pretty okay with that right about now.

The man steps with me, maintaining a position that is far too close to me and directly in my path. "Who are you and what do you want?" I repeat softly. "Answer now or I'll start screaming."

"Is that the typical way you respond to people who wish to speak to you? Screaming?"

"You have ten seconds," I say. "Ten. Nine—"

"Detective Wright," he says. "Consultant for the FBI."

I don't even know what that means but I'm pretty sure it means he's a liar. "Badge," I order.

"Consultant," he repeats, and reaches in his pocket to offer me a card. "That's all you get." My hands are full and he holds it up for me to eye.

"It looks real, but anyone can make a business card."

"Call it in," he says. "But do it after we talk because we're stripped of our privacy." He reaches down and takes my cups, walking to the trash and dumping them. He returns and hands me the card. "Do you know what you're in the middle of, Harper?"

Harper.

The way he uses my first name bothers me. Don't FBI agents usually use your surname? "If you're in a rush to talk to me in private," I say, that very idea setting off warnings, "don't waste time speaking in code."

"Everything is not what it seems and if you don't open your eyes, and see with them, your stepfather won't be the only one in the hospital."

"Is that a threat?"

"It's a fact and a warning. Open your eyes. Look beyond the obvious. Your time is up."

Male voices sound and one of them is Eric's. "Eric!" I call out, and the man in front of me growls low, guttural. He grabs my arm and pulls me to him. "Bitch, you should have waited to hear me out. You should have let me help you. You should have fucking listened to me. Now there's a price to pay."

CHAPTER FORTY-FOUR

Harper

"There's a price to pay," the bearded man rasps at me again.

"Let her go," a female voice hisses, grabbing his arm. The same female who'd crowded me by the supplies. "We have to go," she adds urgently.

The bearded man, the FBI consultant, if I believe his lie, hesitates, but he releases me and then cuts right toward a stairwell. Eric is running toward me, but he's too far to catch the man. The woman darts past me and I reach for her arm but fail. I charge after her. I have to catch her. We have to have answers. We have to end this. I make it all of three steps before Eric grabs my arm and turns me to face him. "What the hell are you doing? Stay here." He's barely spoken the words before he's launching himself forward.

I don't stay. I spy Savage and I need him to know where to go to help Eric and now Eric's around a corner. I start running and reach a turn, rounding the corner just as Eric enters the stairwell, but I make it no further. Savage grabs my arms. "Stop." He turns me to face him. "What the fuck are you doing?"

"Does Eric have a gun?" I demand. "Tell me he has a gun."

"He's got a gun. Talk to me. What just happened?"

"That man told me—"

Eric bursts through the stairwell door. "No one is there. They must have exited a flight up." He eyes Savage. "Get someone looking for them."

Savage grabs his phone and makes a call while Eric crosses the space between us with lightning speed and pulls me to him. "What the hell happened?"

"This man came up to me and he claimed to be FBI. Or a consultant for the FBI. He gave me a card and I'm paraphrasing here but he warned me that I needed to open my eyes. That everything isn't how it seems and if I didn't figure that out, people would die."

Eric scowls. "Holy fuck, why did I let you come to the coffee shop alone?"

"You didn't. I went with Mia and—"

He kisses me, his hand coming down on my head and his tongue licks into my mouth, the taste of fear on his lips. "You go nowhere without me until this is over. Do you understand? Nowhere without me." His voice is low, rough, guttural. "Nowhere, Harper. Do you understand?"

"Yes," I breathe out. "Yes, of course. You don't go anywhere without me either, understand?"

"We stay together," he agrees.

"No one has seen them," Savage interjects, "but we're looking. What the hell are we dealing with here?"

Eric's arm wraps my shoulder, his big body sheltering mine as he turns to face Savage. "Tell him everything. Tell us both everything. Start from the beginning. Pretend I know nothing at all."

I relay every detail I remember about the encounter, down to the color of the man's beard, and Savage is the one scowling when I finish. "FBI? No. We're connected to the FBI. Unless this is a rogue agent, and I doubt he'd have a partner if he was, he wasn't FBI."

Which isn't a surprise to me. I knew he wasn't FBI, and as I stand here now, I'm not rattled the way I was after the warehouse, but I don't take the time to truly analyze that. "He gave me this." I hand Savage the card.

He shoots a picture of it. "I'm texting this to Royce, from our team, who is ex-FBI and well-connected there. I'll have answers for you in about ten minutes." He types a message and sends the photo and then hands me the card.

Eric grabs it and studies it a minute. "What do you want to do right now?" Savage asks. "Stay or go?"

Eric shoves the card into his pocket and turns to me again, his hands on my shoulders. "We go. We'll have Walker deal with the police and our reasons for leaving."

"If they come to the apartment doesn't that bring attention to you by way of bad press that bleeds over to Grayson?"

His lips thin. "We aren't staying. We need to regroup." He eyes Savage and the other man nods and makes a call before he says, "I have men waiting to escort us out when you're ready to leave."

"What about Davis, Mia, and Grayson?" I ask.

"We have a man with them now," Savage assures us. "We'll escort them out of here and stay with them at their homes."

Smith appears right then, and in a few seconds, he's taken up a position behind us while Savage leads the way. Eric keeps me close the entire walk to the elevator, and even inside the elevator car, he uses his big body as a shield. He's afraid of an attack. This man is willing to take a bullet for me. That understanding for me is as good as another proclamation of love, because, yes, he's an ex-SEAL. Yes, he's lived to protect the innocent, but it's more with us. There's a history, a family he hates, and yet, he's always been right here with me, even back on that first night. He warned me away from them. He kissed me and that memory reminded me every day after that there was more out there.

We arrive at the rear door of the hospital and Savage clears the way before we exit. I climb into the backseat of the SUV with Eric by my side. No one is in the driver's seat yet. We're alone and once Eric seals us inside, his fingers tangle into my hair. "You were right earlier. We need to be alone. We need to breathe and we need to do it together." His mouth closes down on mine, his kiss wicked and hungry, an edge to him that I understand. Not once, but twice now, he's come to my rescue. Not once, but twice now, I could have died. I don't know why this hasn't affected me yet. I don't know why it hasn't shaken me to the core, but it has him. I feel that in the way his hand presses between my shoulder blades, molding me close. I feel it in the desperate edge to his kiss.

He's touching me and I'm touching him and it's as if this vehicle doesn't exist. I need him. God, how I need him and my hands slide under his shirt, over warm taut skin, when there's a rap on the window. Eric curses and drags his mouth from mine, his fingers wiping away the dampness there. "Give me just a minute."

"Hurry," I whisper, and somehow my hand is in his pocket closing around that business card I'd given him.

He kisses me again and exits the SUV, shutting the door. I stare down at the card and scoot to a spot where the hospital lights beam down on the writing there. I run my hand over the name and I think again, yes, I was freaked out by that man, especially when he grabbed me but I wasn't afraid in the way I was back in the warehouse. Maybe it was because people were around me and us. Maybe I felt safer; I felt that I had help nearby.

The man's words come back to me: *Everything is not what it seems and if you don't open your eyes, and see with them, your stepfather won't be the only one in the hospital.*

Open my eyes and see with them. As if there's something staring me in the face that I'm ignoring. I flip the card over and my eyes go wide. There's another code on the back, another message. He obviously meant for me to have it, but why not just tell me what it means? Why not just tell me what I need to open my eyes and see?

CHAPTER FORTY-FIVE

Harper

I don't move. I sit there in the SUV, the heater cranked, the soft leather hugging my body, all signaling warmth and comfort, but the card in my hands sends a chill down my spin. No matter what the message on the back of the card means, it spells danger. I stare down at it and read the numbers and letter sequence, trying to find an answer there. The first clue was given to Eric at my house. Now this one was given directly to me. Even I, who am not a savant, can see myself as the common denominator. And that man, the FBI consultant, or whoever he was, told me to open my eyes, as if the answer to some big question is right in front of me. As if I should understand the message. Frustrated, I'm impatient for Eric to return to the vehicle.

I open the door to my right and shove the card into my jacket pocket, aware that we are likely being watched and I don't want anyone to know that I've already discovered the message on the card. The minute I step outside, I find Eric standing a few feet away, not with Savage as I expect, but with Blake, who I didn't even know was here, but the two of them together are exactly the pair I need right now.

Blake to hack the code with a computer.

Eric to hack the code with his mind.

The instant I step onto the curb, the attention of both men shifts to me, their attention sharp, disapproving. They want to shove me back in the SUV. Eric even sways my direction, but I hold up a hand and start walking toward them.

"The card the man gave me," I say without preamble as I join them. "I grabbed it from your pocket and I was looking at it." I shift my gaze between both men. "It had another message on the back. The same kind of message we received back in Denver. Just numbers and letters. I don't want to show you here and risk someone knowing that we've seen the message. It seems like it buys us time to figure it out before they expect some sort of action."

They, I think.

Who are *they*?

We need to find out.

"Good decision," Blake approves, "because while we have to assume the man who gave you that card was an enemy, with this new development, is there a chance that he's actually an informant or friend?"

"The man grabbed her and threatened her," Eric snaps, and apparently just the idea requires that his hand slide around my waist as he pulls me to him. "He's an enemy. The end."

"I guess that means he wasn't FBI?" I ask.

"You guessed right," Blake confirms. "No one at the FBI knows him."

"And on that note," Eric says. "I'm taking her back to the vehicle. I don't want her out in the open until we figure out what the hell is going on."

He doesn't wait for Blake's approval. He starts to turn. "I need a copy of the message," Blake calls out. Eric doesn't stop moving. He simply lifts an agreeable hand and leads me back to the vehicle, his actions protective, possessive. He places me between him and the SUV and then opens the door, his body once again sheltering mine, but I fear for him, not me. That's just it. I'm not scared and maybe that's some mental coping mechanism, a way to block out my warehouse attack. Mia wasn't wrong. Eventually, I'm certain I'll have to face that trauma, but that time isn't now.

I settle into the soft leather of the backseat again and this time when Eric enters, we aren't left alone. Savage joins us almost immediately. "Home?" he asks over his shoulder.

"Yes," Eric replies. "The sooner the better."

Savage places us in motion. "Where's the card?" Eric asks, but before I can respond his cellphone buzzes with a text.

He snakes it from his pocket, eyes the screen as another message pings, and then glances at me. "Adam had to get a doctor in to calm your mother down. She's worried about my father. They gave her Xanax and she's sleeping."

It's then that I step back and realize the hell my mother must be going through. "She lost my father," I say, my hand settling on my knotted belly, "and I've forgotten that to her, this is her worst nightmare. She's preparing to lose the man who became her second partner in life. I've forgotten how much your father means to her." I look at Eric. "She needs me and I've let the poison of this family allow me to forget that."

Eric squeezes my knee. "You're protecting her. *We're* protecting her. Every time you get the chance, you remind me how important protecting her is to you."

"But I wasn't there for her today. I didn't—"

"You were attacked and almost killed. That was less than twenty-four hours ago and even then, you were worried about her. You have not thought of yourself at all. She's safe. The medication will help her cope and as a bonus, the sedation keeps her there with Adam."

"Adam's a badass," Savage chimes in. "This isn't a bad thing. It's good. He'll keep her safe and cozy. They're going to be so safe and cozy they'll have cookies and cocoa when she wakes up. You can bet on it."

I know he's trying to make me laugh. I do and I appreciate it, but it's not going to work. Not when the magnitude of being hunted and forced into hiding has set in. Eric squeezes my knee again and when I don't look at him, he leans into me, his cheek pressing to my cheek, his lips at my ear. "We're going to get through this. We're going to protect your mother."

"But not, I fear, without her suffering," I whisper.

He pulls back to look at me. "Then we'll help her recover." It's not a sugarcoated reply. It doesn't promise me everything is going to be peachy for my mother. She's in love with his father, after all. No one knows more than Eric how much pain his father can cause. No one knows more than Eric that I can't save her from some parts of this.

He strokes a strand of my hair behind my ear, repeating his promise. "We'll help her and we'll do it together. You have my word." His phone buzzes with another text message that he quickly attends to while I savor that word "together" and the raspy, affected tone he'd spoken it in, for just a few seconds longer.

Seconds that end as Eric announces, "Isaac wants to talk." He sticks his phone back in his pocket. "I'm going to let him squirm."

"What if squirming makes him do something stupid?"

Savage chimes in on that one. "Adam will be there to kick his ass and stick a clown hat on him."

I blink. "A clown hat?"

"Yeah," Savage says pulling us to a halt in front of Eric's building. "Issac would look really adorable in a clown hat." He thankfully sets the bad joke aside to add, "Blake said he's waiting on a text from you two."

Eric motions to my pocket. "The card. We need to shoot him a photo of the message on the back."

I hand it to him. He turns it over and when he would shoot a photo, he goes still, suddenly more stone than man. He's just staring at that combination of numbers and letters, and while he's not moving or reacting, I have a sense that it's familiar to him and not in a good way. "What is it?" I ask, grabbing his arm. "What does that mean to you?"

He doesn't look at me. He shoots a photo and sends it to Blake, then sticks his phone and that card inside his pocket. "Let's go upstairs," he says, reaching for the door, and opening it. He actually gets out of the SUV and he's yet to look at me. I'm right. He knows what that message means and it's a problem for him. It's a problem for us. A big enough one that he doesn't want to tell me. Maybe he doesn't plan to tell me at all, but that's not going to fly. He's going to tell me. He's going to tell me the minute we're alone, no matter what kind of new war him and I have to wage.

CHAPTER FORTY-SIX

Harper

Eric and I step into the elevator and Savage actually tries to follow us inside, but I'm not having it. I rotate on him and point. "No. I need to talk to Eric alone. Go take care of the truck or something."

"One of my men—"

"You aren't getting on this elevator, Savage," I say.

He holds up his hands and backs away. The doors shut and Eric keys in the security code to his floor. I rotate to face him. He stares down at me, his eyes hooded, shielding him from my probing stare, and I don't believe this is an accident.

"I know you know what it means." It's all I say, all I can say about the message on the back of the business card when I'm certain that we're being recorded.

His hands come down on my arms and he pulls me to him. "Not here. Not now." His voice is low, rough, an edge to him now that is one-part power, one-part anger, and I'm not sure why.

I rest my palm on the hard wall of his chest, and his heart thunders under my touch. He might seem cool and calm on the outside, but he's not. "You know what it means," I whisper. It's not a question. It's a fact. He knows. I know he knows.

"I know a lot of things," he says. "None of which we're discussing in this elevator."

My eyes narrow on him, on the hard lines of his face, the sharpness to his features I've never noticed until this moment. His defined cheekbones. His square jaw. His steely eyes. "Why are you angry?"

"I have a lot of reasons to be angry, don't you think?"

"Of course, you have reasons, but this, this that you feel right now, is different." The elevator halts and dings, announcing our arrival at our destination, while frustratingly cutting me off before I can press him for more, but it's also the promise of privacy.

The doors open and he takes my hand and starts walking with me, leading me down the hallway toward his apartment. We don't speak, but I can almost feel Eric shutting himself off, caging himself in a place where I don't exist. I'm right. He not only knows what that message means, he doesn't want to tell me. We reach the door and I can't get inside the privacy of his apartment soon enough. What does he know? Why is he this on edge?

He unlocks the door and I quickly walk inside, rotating to face him. "Tell me that message isn't about my mother."

"It's not." He shuts the door, locking it, and then shrugs out of his jacket, hanging it on the coatrack a few feet away, and I get the impression that it's all show. He's avoiding me. He's occupying space that he doesn't want filled with something else.

"That's it?" I press. "You aren't going to say anything else?"

He faces me, his legs spread wide in this alpha, controlling stance, hands settling on his lean hips. "It's not about your mother," he repeats.

He's going to make me ask the question. He's going to make me push. "Then what—"

"It's about me." His statement is hard and flat, and it sits between us like a concrete block.

"You?"

He cuts his gaze, looks skyward, and then to my surprise, he walks away, heading toward the kitchen that connects to the living room.

I shrug out of my jacket and hurry after him tossing it on the couch as I pass it by, and continue my pursuit. Eric rounds the island and opens the fridge. I'm standing with my hand on the island counter, facing him when he shuts the door and removes the cap off a beer. He offers it to me. "It's a good time for a drink."

I don't want the damn beer but I take it. He opens the fridge again and grabs another bottle, twisting off the top, as he had for me. Only this time, when the top is gone, he tips back the beer and downs half of it. I set mine down untouched. "Talk to me. You're scaring me."

He fixes me in a hooded stare, his handsome face all hard lines and shadows, as he orders softly, "Drink the beer, Harper." He downs another swallow of his own.

"I don't want the beer."

He sets his bottle down with a solid thud, then closes the space between us, a predatory intensity about him, as he drags me to him. "Then what do you want?"

"Answers. I want you to talk to me. I want you to—" He tangles rough fingers into my hair and drags my mouth to his.

"No talking," he commands. "Not now. Understand?"

"No," I whisper, his breath warm on my cheek, his body hard against mine. His cock thick against my belly. My sex clenches and my nipples ache. I want him, but this is a distraction. This is him avoiding conversation.

"Eric, please—"

"I like that word," he murmurs, and then he's kissing me, and the first taste of him is passion, the next demand, possession, and yes, anger. He's angry. He's outright pissed for the first time since the hotel room in New York City when he came to me and wanted to drive me away. Only I don't think he ever wanted to drive me away. He wanted to drive away the hell of his past. He wanted to drive away the family he would deny if they'd just go away. He's in that place again. He needs to drive them away, and as much as I want to know what's triggered him, there's a shudder that slides through his body, and I understand what it means. He's on the edge of that cliff the savant in him can drive him to, the numbers in his head beating at his mind and his emotions. Whatever that message I was given says it's personal to him, really damn personal.

My gorgeous, talented, gifted man needs me right now. He needs this escape and I will not deny him. He turns me and presses me against the refrigerator, my back to the steel surface, his hands sliding over my breasts, cupping them, even as his tongue licks into my mouth. I reach for his shirt, but he's already caught the hem of mine and it's over my head in about two seconds. He tosses it and his eyes meet mine, dark shadows in their depths that do nothing to hide the war that rages inside this man.

I want to ask about the message again, I want to ask what it says, what it means, but that is not what he needs right now. That is not what comes next and we both know it. "I know what's happening right now. I know what you're battling. I want to be here for you. What do you need right now?"

"More than I deserve from you."

"What does that even mean?"

"It means I should walk away, but no matter how many times I think that or say that, I won't. I know I won't do it." His body quakes, almost as if he's experiencing an internal tremor that I can physically see.

I press my hand to his chest. "What do you need right now? Right this minute. Say it. Tell me. Take it. Do it."

His hands grip my wrists, and he pulls me close. "You don't want to know what I need right now. You don't want to see me like I am right now. I don't *want* you to see me like I am right now."

"And I don't want you to hide this part of you. *What do you need from me right now*?"

He shuts his eyes, a turbulent, tormented look on his face, his grip almost too hard, but somehow, I wish he'd hold on tighter. "Eric," I whisper.

He opens his eyes and looks at me. "Go to the living room and undress. Wait for me there."

LISA RENEE JONES

CHAPTER FORTY-SEVEN

Harper

"Go to the living room and undress. Wait for me there."

Eric watches me with this command between us. His command to me.

But this isn't about control. I know that instantly. It's about trust and for reasons that stretch beyond the Kingston family, but certainly rooted in their very existence. So yes, his order is daunting, but it's not one that I will refuse him. I don't believe he would ever hurt me. In fact, he's proven that he'll protect me. That he'll include me in his life, down to making the decision to spare his father, the man who he blames for his mother's death. With these things in mind, I don't let him wonder what I would do if I walked into the living room, where I could still back out.

I stand right there in the kitchen and shed every last inch of what I'm wearing down to my socks. Once I'm naked, vulnerable with this man beyond the fact that I'm wearing nothing and he's still dressed, vulnerable in how much I've fallen for him, my chin lifts with a realization. "I don't hesitate with you, Eric," I say. "One day, I hope you won't with me either." And he does hesitate with me. He does automatically package me into a box that he labels "Kingston," which translates to pain. If he didn't, he wouldn't have left me over the baby news. He would

281

have come to me. I press my hand to his chest. "I know you hold back. I know you do, and it's okay. I know what this family has done to you. Just as I know the real love of a family, and I want to be yours."

He stares down at me, his eyes shadowed, hooded, and he doesn't move. He's more stone than man, more muscle than heart. With another realization, I let my hand fall away. He wanted me to go to the living room because he needed a moment to compose himself and step outside whatever savant-related episode he's battling. I might want him to do that with me, I might want to understand this part of him more fully, but he still needs space. I have to understand that.

I step away from him, oblivious now to my naked body. I'm thinking about him. I'm thinking about his walls. I'm thinking about the space between us that this family creates, and while they are why we met, they may well be why we're divided. I make it all of two steps and suddenly he's caught my arm and pulled me back to him. In an inhaled breath, I'm pressed close to him, one of his hands splayed between my shoulder blades, molding my naked chest to his while he tangles the fingers of his free hand into my hair, wrapping the strands tightly, roughly.

"What are you doing to me, woman?"

"What are *you* doing to *me*?"

"I was going to push you. Push you so fucking hard, I probably would have pushed you away."

"Do it. Try. Push me. If that's what you need, if you need to push my limits, and your own, to deal with whatever is going on inside you, then push. I'll push with you. I can handle it."

"Can you?"

"I can handle it. Try me. *Push me.*"

"What if I turn you over my knee? What if I spank you and fuck you and spank you again? What if I take everything that isn't right here with me and destroy it until there is nothing left?"

His words shock but they don't horrify. He's testing me and I understand all the ways he needs to test me. I understand all the reasons he doubts me. I won't fail. "Do it," I challenge and he growls low in his throat.

His phone rings and he grimaces, his mouth coming down on mine, hard, demanding, the taste of anger on his lips all over again. He's angry. He's so very angry and I still don't know why. I sink into the kiss, welcoming the anger, the pain that's hidden deep in the depths of it. The torment I believe he lets me taste. That's his naked truth. That's his path to me and mine to him.

I reach for his T-shirt, and he drags it over his head, tossing it, the logoed cotton that reads "Kingston Motors" somehow appropriately hitting the ground. "Don't wear that shirt again," I order. "It doesn't fit you. And I'm not talking size, and we both know it."

"And it does you?" he demands, his fingers tightening around my hair.

"No. No, it never did, but you do."

I barely finish those words and he's kissing me again, a deep intensity to the stroke of his tongue that is somehow both wild and controlled. I'm wild but not in control. I have this insane feeling I'm about to lose him if I don't get close enough to him, if I don't feel him deep enough. If I don't let him know how much I hunger for him. My hands are all over his body, caressing the taut flesh beneath my palms, that beautiful ink that tells his story, drawing me in, making me hunger for more. I need more. And he touches me and kisses me like he wants all of me, but he already has me.

Somehow I end up on top of the island and Eric's low, rough declaration of, "I need inside you now," has me fumbling with his pants even as he manages to drag them down.

And then he's there, between my legs, thick and hard and pulsing, pressing into the slick wet heat of my body, driving into me, stretching me. He thrusts deep, settling in that deepest spot inside me and for a moment he's staring down at me, studying me like he means to see my soul. "I will push you. I will take more than you want me to take and push you harder than you want to be pushed."

"You can try," I challenge. "But it still won't drive me away."

He cups my face and tilts my mouth to his. "Remember you said that." And then he's kissing me again, taking me in that kiss, and in a thrust of his cock that rockets sensations through me. Taking and taking, but I am, too. I arch into him, lifting my hips, and soon he's cupping my backside, arched over me, forcing my hands to the counter behind me. I'm not oblivious to the control this gives him. I'm not naïve to him needing this, but I want him to have what he needs. I want to heal the hundreds of cuts that bleed from his soul, and I will do anything to make that happen. The way he almost gave everything when he risked his life to save mine in that warehouse.

That is my last coherent thought as sensations rock my body, and his hand cups my breast and pinches my nipple. I arch again, lifting into his thrust and we shatter together, our bodies quaking, trembling and then finally collapsing. We come back to the present with a pounding on the door, and somehow, it feels as if the devil himself is our visitor. Somehow, I just know, maybe because of the fierceness of the pounding, that whatever is on the other side of that door is a problem and not a small one.

CHAPTER FORTY-EIGHT

Harper

I'm still naked on the island, with Eric leaning over me, when yet another pounding sounds on the door. "Is everything okay in there?"

At the sound of Savage's voice, Eric scowls. "Yes," he calls out. "Wait."

"It must be because you didn't answer your phone," I suggest.

"Probably," Eric says, lifting me and setting me on the floor. "Or Savage being Savage and over the top about everything."

I laugh. "There's that, too."

He cups my face. "Sometime soon I'm going to get you alone and keep you naked for an entire weekend but right now, we need to get dressed." He kisses me and when he would release me, I catch his hand.

"Are you okay?"

He cuts his gaze sharply but then he's back, and I'm staring into his clear blue eyes. "With you I am," he says.

It's a reply every woman would welcome from this man, and I do. Of course, I do, but it's not quite a direct answer. It's avoidance I want to poke holes in but I'm naked and Savage is at the door, so I let it go. And for now, only now, I let Eric go, too. He scoops up my clothes and sets them on a barstool. I start dressing as he adjusts his pants, and then grabs his T-shirt. It's then that my gaze catches his tattoos, rows and rows of letters and numbers inking his arms and chest to total completion. Ink that tells his story and that's a story that I don't fully understand yet. Just like the row of letters and numbers on the back of that business card tells a story. One I'm now reminded that Eric understands in some way that I don't. And now, Savage is here to distract us, which isn't well timed. Not when I'm certain that Eric isn't going to share the details he now knows with Savage. He doesn't even want to tell me.

I finish dressing and pull on my socks and shoes to find Eric watching me. "We need to go shopping so you have some things of your own."

I swallow hard, thinking about my home in Denver. Will I go back? Will he stay here? I cut my gaze and Eric is suddenly in front of me. "I don't want you to go back." He pauses as if for effect. "Ever."

This is what I want to hear from him, maybe even needed to hear from him, I realize. I don't want to go back to Denver; I just don't want to leave my mother behind, but as I study this handsome, brilliant man, I set that aside for now. I'm focused on him and the undertone to his words. I'm focused on a hint of trepidation in him, the uncertainty I think I see in his eyes. Does he really think I'd leave him? Does he really think I'm anything but one hundred percent here with him? Yes, I decide. He thinks I'm going to leave, if not now, one day. He thinks I'm somehow too good for him and this tells me that my man, my beautiful man, is so very damaged by this damn family.

There's another knock on the door. "Maybe it's urgent," I say, starting to get concerned. "He knows we're safe now and he's still being pushy."

"Or he's just a pain in my ass," Eric says, already walking toward the door.

I hug myself and step deeper into the kitchen to watch him close the space between us and the entryway, all long-legged grace and confidence, but there's a sharpness to his spine, a tension in his shoulders. The connection between us got him out of his own head, but it was short-lived and we never dealt with whatever set him off.

There's nothing I can do about it now though. Eric's already opening the door and Savage steps inside, and just the brute size of the man is a force when entering a room. "Grayson's in a hired car that just pulled up downstairs," Savage announces, shutting the door. "I tried to call and warn you. We couldn't stop him from coming. He said it's critical that he talk with you."

Eric grimaces, his hands settling on his hips. "I thought you were taking him home?"

"We did," Savage confirms. "He made it all the way into his apartment and then he figured out that you weren't joining him and he wasn't having it. He said he needs to talk to you in private, one on one."

I hug myself a little tighter now and digest this news. Grayson was worried. I know that. He had reason to be worried but this feels over the top. Or is it? Would I let Eric get away with shutting me down if I was worried? No. I wouldn't. Well, outside of sex on the kitchen island, which distracted me, but that wasn't meant to replace conversation. And yet it has. I can't talk to him now.

Eric runs a hand through his hair, an act of utter frustration that he rarely displays. He's a man of control and between myself and Grayson, we're practically wrestling it from his grip. That can't sit well. "Bring him up when he gets here."

Savage's phone buzzes with a text message and he glances at it and then Eric. "That would be now."

Eric's lips thin. "Of course it is. Is Mia with him?"

287

"No. Grayson made her stay with one of our men and," he glances at me and then Eric again, "he seems to really want to talk to you alone."

Eric turns away from Savage and just leaves him standing there. He walks right by me, through the living, to the bar area just beside his patio door. Shutting us out, claiming an empty space that I believe he lives inside far too often. Eager to fill that space, I cross to join him, watching as he pours himself a drink.

"Talk to me," I whisper, aware of Savage nearby, and wishing he'd just step back into the hallway.

"Not now," he says softly, and he still doesn't look at me. "Later."

The doorbell rings and he downs his drink, setting the glass on the bar before he turns to me, his hand cupping my neck as he drags his mouth to mine. "There's much unsaid and undone between us, too much, but not for long." He kisses me, a deep, drugging kiss that is over too soon. Suddenly, he's set me aside, and he's gone, his long legs eating away the space between him and the door again.

Something in his words, in his manner, guts me, cuts me, burns me but I can do nothing but feel his pain. I can't stop it. Not now, and part of me wonders if I'll ever be able to. I pour myself a drink and down it, another type of burn—the whiskey-induced kind—following, settling in my belly. I might regret that decision later, but right now I need to come down. I turn as Grayson and Eric enter the living room. "Harper," Grayson greets.

"Hey, Grayson," I say and without further preamble, I add, "I know you two need to talk. I'll go upstairs."

"We'll step into my office," Eric replies. "You stay here if you like. We won't be long."

They won't be long. Eric doesn't want to talk to Grayson anymore than he does me. I nod and the two men cross the living room and enter the office, the same office where Eric had cursed out Smith for leaving the door unguarded. I wonder who is at the door now. I wonder what it would be like to live without this kind of drama, without the Kingston imprint on our lives. I watch Eric and Grayson disappear into the room and shut themselves away. Once I'm fully alone, I pour a splash more of whiskey into my glass and down it, choking with the burn that slides along my throat.

Once I arrive at Eric's bedroom, I pause at the doorway to stare at the massive bed, his bed. The bed he wants me to share with him again tonight. I'm so deeply entrenched in this man's life and he in mine, that there's no turning back. Whatever comes next, no matter how good or bad, it's in motion. I inhale with the odd sense of foreboding that follows, rejecting it entirely. I'm here with Eric. He's got men protecting my mother. We're okay. We will stay okay.

Entering the room, I sit down on the chair in front of the window, staring forward without really seeing what's beyond the glass. Eric's voice lifts through the vent on the floor by the wall. "The bearded man gave her this," I hear him say, and I assume that Eric's now handing Grayson the card. "We received a similar message in Denver."

"From who?" Grayson asks. "The bearded man? He was there, too?"

"A different man. He parked in front of her house. When I approached him, he drove away and threw a message out of his window."

"Numbers and letters," Grayson says. "It reads like a message to you but this message seemed to target her. Was the other one the same?"

"Same format, different letters and numbers."

I stand up. I shouldn't be listening. I need to just leave the room, but then Grayson says, "What do they mean?" And that question plants my feet.

"Yes," I whisper. "What do they mean to you, Eric?"

"I haven't figured out the first one," Eric replies to Grayson. "But this one, the one Harper was handed at the hospital. This one is personal."

"Explain," Grayson presses and I hold my breath, waiting for what comes next, my stomach in knots.

"It translates to a saying we had in the SEALs. *If you ain't cheating, you ain't trying.* It means to win, you have to break the rules."

Grayson's silent for several beats and I imagine him studying Eric, before he says, "And you think that means someone knows what rules you were going to break with Kingston."

"Don't you?" Eric challenges. "It's a fucking threat. They want me to do something for them, pay them off in some way, or they'll tell Harper."

"Then you tell Harper. That's why I came here. You have to tell her."

"Tell her I betrayed her? Tell her I lied to her? Hell no. That's not happening."

"We both know it's not that simple. Explain it to her but tell her. Before someone else tells her."

Not because he loves me, I think. Not because he trusts me. Because someone else might tell me. Because someone else knows. This reasoning guts me more than the secret, the lie, that is obviously between me and Eric.

"She'll walk away," Eric bites out, his voice low, rough, guttural, "and I can't, *I cannot*, let her walk away."

And I can't breathe.

I can't breathe and my heart is beating so fast that I feel like I'm going to pass out. The voices go silent, or my heartbeat blasts over them, I don't know which. I don't even remember the moment that I exit the bedroom. I don't remember the walk down the stairs. I'm just standing at the office door. I open it and Eric and Grayson turn to me.

"I was upstairs. I heard you talking. I wasn't trying to, but—" I turn to Eric. "Tell me. Tell me everything. Is nothing between us real? Is this all a lie? Why can't you afford to let me walk away, Eric? What is this really all about?"

The end...for now

Readers,
Thank you so much for picking up THE PRINCESS! Harper and Eric's story concludes very soon in THE EMPIRE which is available for pre-order on all platforms now!

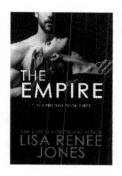

PRE-ORDER AND LEARN MORE HERE:
http://filthytrilogy.lisareneejones.com

IN THE MOOD FOR A COWBOY ROMANCE?

THE TRUTH ABOUT COWBOYS is coming out this year in mass market paperback (in stores everywhere!) and ebook on August 27, 2019!

https://www.goodreads.com/book/show/43582158-the-truth-about-cowboys

WANT MORE LISA RENEE JONES ROMANCE?

Have you read my Dirty Rich series? A series of super sexy lawyers filled with passion and mystery! Check it out here:

http://dirtyrich.lisareneejones.com

NEW STANDALONE COMING IN MY LILAH LOVE SERIES!

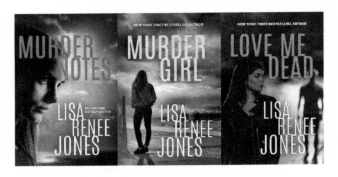

This series is a suspense series with a steamy side of romance! The first two books are available now, but the third book can be read as a standalone as well!

https://www.lilahlove.com/

A NEW PSYCHOLOGICAL THRILLER COMING SOON!

A PERFECT LIE is definitely far and away from what I usually write, but I am so excited about it! I hope you'll check it out!

https://aperfectliebook.weebly.com

ALSO BY LISA RENEE JONES

THE INSIDE OUT SERIES

If I Were You
Being Me
Revealing Us
His Secrets*
Rebecca's Lost Journals
The Master Undone*
My Hunger*
No In Between
My Control*
I Belong to You
All of Me*

THE SECRET LIFE OF AMY BENSEN

Escaping Reality
Infinite Possibilities
Forsaken
Unbroken*

CARELESS WHISPERS

Denial
Demand
Surrender

WHITE LIES

Provocative
Shameless

TALL, DARK & DEADLY

Hot Secrets
Dangerous Secrets
Beneath the Secrets

WALKER SECURITY

Deep Under
Pulled Under
Falling Under

LILAH LOVE

Murder Notes
Murder Girl
Love Me Dead (2019)

DIRTY RICH

Dirty Rich One Night Stand
Dirty Rich Cinderella Story
Dirty Rich Obsession
Dirty Rich Betrayal
Dirty Rich Cinderella Story: Ever After
Dirty Rich One Night Stand: Two Years Later
Dirty Rich Obsession: All Mine

THE FILTHY TRILOGY

The Bastard
The Princess
The Empire (March 2019)

*eBook only

ABOUT THE AUTHOR

New York Times and USA Today bestselling author Lisa Renee Jones is the author of the highly acclaimed INSIDE OUT series.

In addition to the success of Lisa's INSIDE OUT series, she has published many successful titles. The TALL, DARK AND DEADLY series and THE SECRET LIFE OF AMY BENSEN series, both spent several months on a combination of the New York Times and USA Today bestselling lists. Lisa is also the author of the bestselling the bestselling LILAH LOVE and WHITE LIES series.

Prior to publishing, Lisa owned multi-state staffing agency that was recognized many times by The Austin Business Journal and also praised by the Dallas Women's Magazine. In 1998 Lisa was listed as the #7 growing women owned business in Entrepreneur Magazine.

Lisa loves to hear from her readers. You can reach her on Twitter and Facebook daily.

CPSIA information can be obtained
at www.ICGtesting.com
Printed in the USA
LVHW041952060219
606614LV00001B/38/P